The Black Sultan

SELECTED FICTION WORKS BY
L. RON HUBBARD

A full list of L. Ron Hubbard's
novellas and short stories is provided at the back.

*Dekalogy—a group of ten volumes

L. RON HUBBARD

The Black Sultan

GALAXY
PRESS

Published by
Galaxy Press, LLC
7051 Hollywood Boulevard, Suite 200
Hollywood, CA 90028

Printed in the United States of America.

ISBN-10 1-59212-353-8
ISBN-13 978-1-59212-353-7

Library of Congress Control Number: 2007903605

Contents

Stories from Pulp Fiction's Golden Age

A ND it *was* a golden age.
The 1930s and 1940s were a vibrant, seminal time for a gigantic audience of eager readers, probably the largest per capita audience of readers in American history. The magazine racks were chock-full of publications with ragged trims, garish cover art, cheap brown pulp paper, low cover prices—and the most excitement you could hold in your hands.

"Pulp" magazines, named for their rough-cut, pulpwood paper, were a vehicle for more amazing tales than Scheherazade could have told in a million and one nights. Set apart from higher-class "slick" magazines, printed on fancy glossy paper with quality artwork and superior production values, the pulps were for the "rest of us," adventure story after adventure story for people who liked to *read*. Pulp fiction authors were no-holds-barred entertainers—real storytellers. They were more interested in a thrilling plot twist, a horrific villain or a white-knuckle adventure than they were in lavish prose or convoluted metaphors.

The sheer volume of tales released during this wondrous golden age remains unmatched in any other period of literary history—hundreds of thousands of published stories in over nine hundred different magazines. Some titles lasted only an issue or two; many magazines succumbed to paper shortages during World War II, while others endured for decades yet. Pulp fiction remains as a treasure trove of stories you can read, stories you can love, stories you can remember. The stories were driven by plot and character, with grand heroes, terrible villains, beautiful damsels (often in distress), diabolical plots, amazing places, breathless romances. The readers wanted to be taken beyond the mundane, to live adventures far removed from their ordinary lives—and the pulps rarely failed to deliver.

In that regard, pulp fiction stands in the tradition of all memorable literature. For as history has shown, good stories are much more than fancy prose. William Shakespeare, Charles Dickens, Jules Verne, Alexandre Dumas—many of the greatest literary figures wrote their fiction for the readers, not simply literary colleagues and academic admirers. And writers for pulp magazines were no exception. These publications reached an audience that dwarfed the circulations of today's short story magazines. Issues of the pulps were scooped up and read by over thirty million avid readers each month.

Because pulp fiction writers were often paid no more than a cent a word, they had to become prolific or starve. They also had to write aggressively. As Richard Kyle, publisher and editor of *Argosy*, the first and most long-lived of the pulps, so pointedly explained: "The pulp magazine writers, the best of them, worked for markets that did not write for critics or attempt to satisfy timid advertisers. Not having to answer to anyone other than their readers, they wrote about human beings on the edges of the unknown, in those new lands the future would explore. They wrote for what we would become, not for what we had already been."

Some of the more lasting names that graced the pulps include H. P. Lovecraft, Edgar Rice Burroughs, Robert E. Howard, Max Brand, Louis L'Amour, Elmore Leonard, Dashiell Hammett, Raymond Chandler, Erle Stanley Gardner, John D. MacDonald, Ray Bradbury, Isaac Asimov, Robert Heinlein—and, of course, L. Ron Hubbard.

In a word, he was among the most prolific and popular writers of the era. He was also the most enduring—hence this series—and certainly among the most legendary. It all began only months after he first tried his hand at fiction, with L. Ron Hubbard tales appearing in *Thrilling Adventures, Argosy, Five-Novels Monthly, Detective Fiction Weekly, Top-Notch, Texas Ranger, War Birds, Western Stories,* even *Romantic Range.* He could write on any subject, in any genre, from jungle explorers to deep-sea divers, from G-men and gangsters, cowboys and flying aces to mountain climbers, hard-boiled detectives and spies. But he really began to shine when he turned his talent to science fiction and fantasy of which he authored nearly fifty novels or novelettes to forever change the shape of those genres.

Following in the tradition of such famed authors as Herman Melville, Mark Twain, Jack London and Ernest Hemingway, Ron Hubbard actually lived adventures that his own characters would have admired—as an ethnologist among primitive tribes, as prospector and engineer in hostile climes, as a captain of vessels on four oceans. He even wrote a series of articles for *Argosy*, called "Hell Job," in which he lived and told of the most dangerous professions a man could put his hand to.

Finally, and just for good measure, he was also an accomplished photographer, artist, filmmaker, musician and educator. But he was first and foremost a *writer*, and that's the L. Ron Hubbard we come to know through the pages of this volume.

This library of Stories from the Golden Age presents the best of L. Ron Hubbard's fiction from the heyday of storytelling, the Golden Age of the pulp magazines. In these eighty volumes, readers are treated to a full banquet of 153 stories, a kaleidoscope of tales representing every imaginable genre: science fiction, fantasy, western, mystery, thriller, horror, even romance—action of all kinds and in all places.

Because the pulps themselves were printed on such inexpensive paper with high acid content, issues were not meant to endure. As the years go by, the original issues of every pulp from *Argosy* through *Zeppelin Stories* continue crumbling into brittle, brown dust. This library preserves the L. Ron Hubbard tales from that era, presented with a distinctive look that brings back the nostalgic flavor of those times.

L. Ron Hubbard's Stories from the Golden Age has something for every taste, every reader. These tales will return you to a time when fiction was good clean entertainment and the most fun a kid could have on a rainy afternoon or the best thing an adult could enjoy after a long day at work. Pick up a volume, and remember what reading is supposed to be all about. Remember curling up with a *great story.*

—Kevin J. Anderson

KEVIN J. ANDERSON *is the author of more than ninety critically acclaimed works of speculative fiction, including* The Saga of Seven Suns, *the continuation of the* Dune Chronicles *with Brian Herbert, and his* New York Times *bestselling novelization of L. Ron Hubbard's* Ai! Pedrito!

The Black Sultan

CHAPTER ONE

El Zidan

THEIR medals were clinking, their rowels spun on the upward-curving pavement, their scarlet breeches put to shame the tropical brilliance of the Moroccan town. Encased in shining leather were their revolvers, gold lanyards attached. They had stopped now, looking at me.

It was hard to sit there at a sidewalk table and idly spin a glass between thumb and forefinger—as hard as trying to keep an agonized finger on a hot stove.

The taller of the two unfastened his holster flap and stabbed a knowing glance at his companion. They were Legion officers on leave, but they knew their duty to Morocco, to France.

How easy it would have been for me to drag the .45 from against my ribs and give it to them. But something of the fatality of the situation was with me. Although I did not consciously realize it, I was at a crossroads of life and three factors were bearing down upon me, converging. To crush me between them, quite probably.

Evidently, the taller of the two saw the threat in my eyes. He called out, "*Americain!* I, Captain Nicolle, order you to stand up and come here."

He needn't have announced himself. I remembered him from a past visit to this place, just as he knew me—however vaguely.

It was useless to disobey. The eight-thousand-mile trek was over. Eddie Moran was through. France had caught up with me.

As I started to rise, a hail came from across the street: "Hey! Hey! Hey! Eddie Moran! Wait for me!"

Two men were coming down a twisty flight of stairs. I recognized the first as Godfrey Harrison, United States vice-consul. His companion was unknown to me—and that was strange, since he looked important and I should have known him as I knew the country. I experienced a wish to meet him.

The stranger was tall and brawny. White silk djellaba flowing about him like a whirlpool of cream, red turban wound aslant above a large, lean face, he came down the steps with an easy stride which made you think of kings.

Once more I was about to obey Nicolle's command when I heard the grunt of camels behind me. A caravan was swinging down the narrow street, filling it to overflowing. Townspeople scurried out of the way, hugging the walls to allow the caravan passage.

I heaved a sigh of relief. The caravan would pass between me and the officers and that would give me all the time I required. Smiling, I looked up at the desert riders who swung toward me in a blaze of color.

They must belong to some great man, I thought, judging by their military bearing and the excellence of their equipment. Once more I was baffled as to identity. Things had changed since I had last been here. Things had grown much more complicated, too.

Once more I thought I could save my bacon. The French had put me down as a highly dangerous gentleman. They classed me in the same breath with revolutionists, gunfighters, smugglers, and anything else they thought was vile.

In saving myself from them before, I had been forced to shoot my way out—I don't know how often. In trying to nail me down, they had forced me to become what they thought I was.

In that second, the Moroccan sunlight became bright again. I forgot about the French and about Godfrey Harrison. I felt as though someone had exploded an AVB rifle grenade in my chest.

Just a pair of eyes, infinitely cool, infinitely deep, looking at me quite impersonally from behind a veil. Just a few strands of gold escaping from the jeweled headpiece. Just a girl mounted on a swaying camel. But I'll never forget how she looked when I saw her then, that first time.

"*Americain!*" bawled *Capitaine* Nicolle. "Put up—"

As swift as striking snakes, hands darted for gun boots. A scimitar flashed like silver lightning and the barbs lunged forward—straight toward Godfrey Harrison!

I thought for an instant that I would see a dead vice-consul. It was inevitable. It had happened too fast. And I was as surprised as the others when the .45 Colt came away from my ribs and started to jar my palm.

A scimitar was coming down. As well as I could, I spotted the base of the djellaba hood and fired. The man reared up straight. The sword clanged against the pavement and the Berber came tumbling out of his saddle limply.

5

The other Berber whirled about, trying to level his Snider. He caught a bullet in his teeth and I saw the sick roll of his eyes as he began to slide down.

I was aware, standing wreathed in my own powder smoke, that the girl was staring at me, not at the dead men. Camel boys tugged at their halters and the caravan plunged down the curving street.

A hawk-faced rider paused, saw me raise the gun, and thought better of valor. He was lost in the welter of dust which rose from escaping hoofs.

The two French officers were still there, pressed back against a wall like life-size toy soldiers. I suppose they thought they were next.

Godfrey Harrison swabbed at the sweatband of his pith helmet and tottered across to me.

"My God, Eddie," he quavered, "that was close! But why, oh why did you do it? You're in hot water now—bad enough without all that."

Behind Harrison came the silk-robed gentleman, face impassive. His fingers rested lightly on the tip of his blond beard and I thought I saw a twinkle in his blue eyes.

Deciding they were not to be targets, the two Frenchmen bristled and strode up. *Capitaine* Nicolle was snorting like a winded horse.

"Ah, so that is it!" cried Nicolle. "You destroy the peace of Morocco. You carry dangerous weapons. You attack our citizens without provocation. Now, *Americain*, we will send you back."

"Back where?" I demanded.

The other Berber whirled about, trying to level his Snider.
He caught a bullet in his teeth and I saw the sick roll
of his eyes as he began to slide down.

He pried my fingers off my gun and took it from me. "Back to French Indochina! We know you, so do not pretend. You are that so infamous Edward Moran, enemy of France. Ah, but we have orders concerning you!"

The big tribesman stepped easily forward. "Allow me," he said in French, "to introduce myself."

With an insolence only a Frenchman can achieve, they turned their backs upon him and fastened upon my arms.

I planted my boot heels and balked. Godfrey Harrison swabbed anew at his sweatband and sputtered.

"I say," mourned Godfrey. "You can't do that, you know. He's an American citizen and—"

I wonder why it is most of our consuls in faraway spots must affect a British accent.

They paid no attention whatever to Harrison, and his eyes were sad and watery behind the spectacles perched on his thin nose. The officers were putting their backs to the task. My heels were skidding, raising small whirlpools of dust. Berbers stopped and watched, crowding to obtain grandstand seats.

The Legion officers were rumpled. They loosed their holds and stepped back straightening their tunics, realizing, doubtless, that a street fight lay far beneath their dignity. After a moment's deliberation Nicolle drew his stumpy revolver and centered the muzzle on my chest.

"Now march!" he commanded. "We do not have to fuss with you, Moran."

"Nor I with you," I replied, dusting my hands and looking at the gun. I hate to be pawed and my temper was rising. "You haven't any order for my arrest."

"Ho!" cried the little one, gazing all about him in mock surprise. "He thinks we need an order for his arrest. He thinks such a victim of Madame Guillotine needs warrants and process of law. He thinks—"

"Hah," echoed the other, "he is crazy. All *Americains* are crazy. He organizes a revolt against France and then escapes, and now—"

"I didn't organize a revolt!" I protested. "I convoyed three Annamite chiefs up the Magat in a speedboat." Which was true. I had also helped them drill their little yellow soldiers, but I hoped France would not know that.

"You came," said the tallest, "on a Trans-African Airliner. You go back by narrow gauge railroad, third class. By that, and in the hold of a smelly tramp. If you manage to arrive alive, you will be executed, but perhaps we should save France that expense."

The big blond stepped up again. He laid firm hands on the epaulets of the two and gently lifted them apart.

"Pardon my intrusion, gentlemen, but my name is El Zidan." He said it so quietly you knew that it meant a great deal.

The Frenchmen gaped. The little one made a noise like a throttled crow.

"El Zidan? But El Zidan is—is—You cannot come like this, openly, to town—"

"I am here," said El Zidan. "That caravan was the property of Abu 'l Hasan, the Black Sultan." He motioned with a disdainful finger at the two lumps of cloth and blood which lay upon the pavement, attracting flies.

"Those men," continued El Zidan, "saw me and knew me. They tried to kill me by riding me down. This Eddie Moran saw it in time, and acted quickly, saving my life. Therefore I intercede for him, and should you gentlemen see fit to make an issue of it, I'm afraid that no more horses will be sent to *la belle Légion*. You are the judge."

The Frenchmen looked too stunned to move, but they managed to salute. Their scarlet pants walked away from there in a military straight line.

Nicolle went about thirty feet and then came back. He shook a finger under my nose and strained his words through his teeth.

"All right, *mon ami*. All right! You have a champion this time. But we have an additional charge against you for killing two men, and carrying concealed weapons. *Monsieur* Moran, I give you twenty-four hours to get out of the town! After that, a Legion patrol will pick you up and throw you in jail awaiting extradition." He glanced at El Zidan. "Horses or no horses!"

CHAPTER TWO

The Offer

H E went away after that and our eyes followed his straight back out of sight. "A stickler for duty, that Nicolle," said El Zidan in drawling English. "He will do as he says."

Smiling, he seated himself at my table and hitched at two cartridge belts which girded his loins. In the holsters were guns unlike anything I had ever seen. Flat, blue automatics with butts chased in silver and gold. The cartridges looked like platinum against polished leather.

"Close!" Godfrey was muttering and mopping. "Close— My word, Eddie, why did you come to this country, of all places?"

"I didn't think they'd look for me," I said. "How was I to know that my picture had been shipped around? And as for coming here, Harrison, that's simple. I'm broke. I had just enough money to buy a Trans-African Airline ticket this far. And I said to myself, 'My old pal, my college chum, my old buddy Godfrey Harrison is vice-consul down there. And I've never seen Godfrey Harrison without money. It clings to his fingers.'"

Harrison sputtered. "But my dear old fellow, I can't be seen aiding a fugitive from justice. Think of my position! Little did I suppose that anything like this would be hanging over your head when you radioed me to meet you here. After all, my dear old fellow!"

"I was thinking about your position," I said. "You're going to fake me a passport so I can leave this burg. I can't get out without a passport, even though I got in without one."

"Eddie," he said severely, "you are always getting into messes like this. You're well educated and personable. You could gain a position with any large oil firm. But you are always in trouble. You could even be a consul, my dear fellow. And here you are—here you are without a coat!

"An American with no coat and no tie! Dressed in riding breeches and riding boots. Carrying a gun inside your shirt! And a white felt hat. Haven't you even a pith helmet?"

"No badges of dignity," I had to admit. "But I'll buy them when you lend me five hundred dollars. Listen, Harrison, I know a fellow in Argentina who has a good thing. He says that we could raise about two thousand men and a—"

Harrison sighed so forlornly that I stopped. I did not know whether he sighed for me or for his five hundred dollars.

El Zidan chuckled soundlessly and pulled his blond beard.

"Moran, you fascinate me," he said. I blinked, staring at him. It suddenly struck me that his English savored of Oxford. "Yes," he continued, "you fascinate me. Were you a—a—cowboy in the United States?"

"Cowboy? Why so?"

"But I thought all you men were cowboys in the United States. I have seen motion pictures in London which—" He stopped, a little surprised at my laughter.

"You laugh at the motion pictures?" wondered El Zidan.

"But I thought they were marvelous. Men riding along on horses shooting at cow thieves. I've often thought I would like to go there. You see, Moran, I am quite indebted to the motion pictures."

It was my turn to blink. But he swept on in his deep, drawling voice:

"I now have a profession where before I had only a rather shaky title."

Harrison tried to head him off, but El Zidan was very absorbed in his subject.

"You see, when I grew up," continued El Zidan, "and found out that I was really heir to a throne in the High Atlas, I tried to think of every possible way to annoy Abu 'l Hasan, the usurper. But it was not until I found that horses could be—could be—could be rustled as well as cows that I hit upon my—"

"Don't you think—" began Harrison.

El Zidan did not so much as glance at the vice-consul:

"—And so, the Black Sultan is extremely annoyed, vastly harassed and generally discomforted."

I studied the man's face to see if he was serious. The blue eyes were twinkling, but he was obviously in earnest. The statements he had made came home to me, and my one bad habit is laughing at the wrong time.

Here was a man dressed in silk and red leather, with a pair of automatics worth a sultan's ransom, telling me that he was a horse rustler.

He began to laugh with me, and the creamy, silken cloak rippled. His tremendous shoulders shook and his voice boomed like the surf. Suddenly he stopped and climbed to his feet. I got up with him and discovered that he was about my height and general build.

"We go now," he said, holding out his hand.

When I had extricated my palm from his grip I remembered. "Wait. Tell me. There was a girl in that caravan. She looked like an English girl. Blue eyes and gold hair. Does—"

"Probably Berber," said El Zidan. "Like myself, many of the upper-class Berbers are Hamitic."

Harrison edged nervously away, probably thinking about the five hundred. El Zidan still lingered.

"Moran," he said, setting his jaws, "I have an idea that you are not going to leave Morocco."

"No?"

"No. The French have an odd code of ethics. You have wronged them, so they think, and rather than embarrass themselves and earn my wrath, I believe you will be found stabbed to death in a gutter tomorrow morning."

"You're encouraging."

"I tell you because I am greedy, Moran. Frankly, I want to scare you into accepting my offer."

"I frighten easily," I assured him.

His teeth flashed in a grin.

"I can see that," he laughed. "You come with me, Moran, and in a short time I'll make you vizier—grand vizier—of a kingdom as big as your New England states."

Of course a man in my position and profession thinks in terms of kingdoms. But the way he said it jolted me. Before I could answer he pumped my hand again.

"Go to the Wagon-Lit—the only one here fit for a gentleman—and reserve the best suite of rooms. Stay there, charge anything you want to me. Tomorrow morning you will hear from me. I leave for the High Atlas tonight."

His djellaba swirled and his red boots rang against the stones. He strode after Harrison, shoulders swinging, his red turban standing out against the white and green of the street like a shining drop of blood.

I pulled my felt hat down over my eyes and tramped toward the hotel.

In the morning, in the chill post-dawn hour, they woke me with coffee and toast at my bedside. New clothes were laid out and the shower was already running.

When I started down the wide staircase, the manager bounded up to me with undignified agility.

"No, no," he hissed. "Not the front way! A squadron of cavalry are waiting. El Zidan would never forgive me if I let you walk through danger unwarned."

"But my twenty-four hours," I began.

"I know nothing of twenty-four hours. The French officers cannot count. The back way, *Monsieur*! I am desolated that you must walk through garbage, but—"

He led me down another flight. I saw no garbage. Instead everything was as magnificent as the front way, though on a smaller scale.

Leading me down steps into a garden, quiet and spicy in the fresh morning air, he paused and spread his hand toward the fountain. I promptly forgot about the manager.

Standing there was an Arabian stallion, head up, eyes alive.

15

He was glossy white and the giant muscles of his chest rippled as he pawed restlessly at the flagstones. He was a tremendous beast, built for speed.

Upon his back an Arabian saddle was cinched. It was made of polished red leather inlaid with sparkling gold conchas the size of saucers. The skirts were outlined in rows of translucent stones, which caught and held the chilly sunlight.

Across the cantle lay a djellaba, a turban and a pair of holsters. A little surprised, I picked them off and examined them. The hooded cloak was creamy satin, lined with scarlet. The turban was a brilliant red. The automatics—

I looked long at those automatics, taking them out of the holsters and turning them over and over and getting drunker by the second.

These were El Zidan's guns!

Slightly dazed by the brilliant show, I sat back on a bench and stared at the stallion. I became aware of an arrogant Berber.

"El Zidan has sent you," he intoned, "his horse, his turban, his djellaba and his guns. You are to join him in the High Atlas with all haste."

The solid world where fact is fact settled back upon me.

"Just where in the High Atlas?" I demanded.

The Berber, still unbending, said, "That, even El Zidan does not know."

"But the High Atlas—" I sighed so mournfully that the Arabian pricked up his ears. It had suddenly struck me that I might as well be told that El Zidan would be found in the Rocky Mountains.

I tossed the cloak about my shoulders and felt it float down into place. I wrapped the scarlet turban about my head and pinned it with a diamond clasp. I buckled on the jewelry and thrust a foot into the stirrup.

The stallion snorted and dodged, but when I eased myself solidly into the saddle, he turned and eyed me as much as to say, "I just wanted to know, that's all."

The Berber said a few words—but a jarring clatter of sabers and hoofs drowned his voice.

There was not even time to register surprise. An officer mounted on a lathered sorrel appeared like a *jinnī* in the gate. Behind him a troop of native cavalry came to a clamorous halt.

I jerked the stallion's reins and his breath whistled sharply between his teeth. His forefeet came up and pawed the air while I clung with my knees to the saddle.

The expression on the officer's face changed. "El Zidan!" he exclaimed. "But Nicolle—"

"Be damned to Nicolle!" I cried. "Clear your offal away! I cannot be detained."

They swerved to the right and left and the stallion trotted through them. I held my head low, hoping to get away with it. But the officer's eyes were too sharp for me. He evidently had had dealings with El Zidan.

He cried, "You're not—! Get him! It's the *Americain!*"

I roweled the white flanks. The stallion threw out his feet, hammering stone. The walls swept away in a swift blur. A carbine rapped sharply. A glance over my shoulder was enough to convince me that they were in earnest. A gaudy blob of racing color was hanging to my heels.

17

A glance over my shoulder was enough to convince me that they were in earnest. A gaudy blob of racing color was hanging to my heels.

Once more I raked the flank with spur. The Arabian stretched himself. We rocketed around the corner of a house and lunged through a twisting street. People shrieked as they sprang for the walls.

Ahead I saw a gate and two sentries. In all this deafening clamor of hoofs and cries I distinctly heard an order, bawled from a guardhouse.

"It's the *Americain*! Shoot him!"

They knew, I suppose, that native cavalry would not chase El Zidan. One sentry dropped on his knee and threw up his Lebel, as precisely as though on a rifle range. The flame was white in the sunshine.

But the stallion had evidently been through this before. He cleared the soldier, jumped all the way over his head. The hard hillside was under us, flowing past like a tan river. The blob of color was less distinct.

CHAPTER THREE

The Palace

EACH night found me higher, found the air thinner, found the grass scarcer and the food harder to get. Villagers were not unfriendly, but sometimes when they thought I slept I caught them peering at me with inquisitive eyes. Their hospitality was as good as their religion—even though religion is a matter of convenience to a Berber.

The stallion was an untiring machine with pistons for legs. No slope was too steep, no ravine too deep, no mountain pass too sharply twisting.

In the tawny blackness of the High Atlas the nights were bitter. And in this season—spring—occasional snow came padding down, filling up the defiles, impeding my progress.

I had a fair idea of my destination and I felt that a lookout would pick me up when I neared El Zidan's camp.

One afternoon as we trotted between boulders and around conifers, I caught a glimpse of a staccato sparkle far ahead and above me. I reined in and watched.

The dot appeared and disappeared with swift regularity.

After a moment's study I knew that it was a heliograph. I tried Morse, but that was not the code. It should have cheered me, that talking sunlight, but it did not. It felt very cold. And had I been adept at forecasting events I would have turned the stallion down the mountain side and plunged away toward the coast.

But I did not know, and I sat there thinking that this was El Zidan signaling a sentry to pick me up and bring me into the camp.

Riding on, I searched the rocks ahead for a sign of greeting, but it was not until I had ridden for more than an hour that I spotted the rider.

He was sitting on a barb in the shadow of a giant oak, his eyes restless as he watched my approach, his right hand hidden in his djellaba.

I drew in and held up my arm in salute. He did not return the greeting. Feeling as though I had offered my hand to a man who disdained to shake it, I let the stallion walk in closer. The Berber's hand came into sight and with it came a Webley pistol.

"I'm a friend!" I called out in French.

He did not seem to hear. The revolver had the appearance of a train tunnel.

"Advance," he said. "Slowly or I send thee with all despatch to *Shaitan*."

His eyes were searching my face. Little by little surprise seeped into his expression. Finally he cried:

"You're not—" He laughed and put away the gun. "Come," he said. "You're among friends. For a moment I thought you must be an officer of the Black Sultan."

Perhaps if I were more clever than I am I would have reasoned that El Zidan's sentry would know El Zidan's cloak.

But I was so immensely relieved to see the gun go back to its holster that I waved everything else aside.

He guided his barb alongside me and we rode up the pass. "We will be in camp presently," he said conversationally. "After that we will amuse ourselves one way and another. My master is very anxious to see you."

"And I to see him," I replied. "Is it far?"

"Not far. There are others ahead who have come out to escort you in."

A stranger in a new country is at a very decided disadvantage. All people of the new race look alike to him and because of that he does not remember faces. Still, the more I looked at this dark skinned Berber the more I thought I had seen him elsewhere. Probably he had been close to El Zidan that afternoon in the street.

The sun was almost gone when we met the others. They were silent men, ghosts in grey djellabas. They drifted out of the rocks and guided their horses close to the stallion on either flank. No word was spoken and as I glanced about me, I sensed a tension in their bodies and expressions which made me uneasy. I had no reason for the feeling and I tried to brush it aside.

But that did not deter me from noticing that their eyes never left me, that their hands were close to their belts, that they carried their guns loaded and cocked.

Night settled, a dark, drifting fog. The sunlight turned crimson and then old rose. And the slow hoofbeats of the barbs about me went on like ticking metronomes.

Two riders swung closer and closer to my sides, watching my hands and not the path ahead. We had been passing through broken country, but now the trail had wormed in between two cliffs from which there was no escape. It was necessary to continue as the path dictated.

The riders about me were faint blurs of white in the darkness, moving easily.

It came to me then that I was a prisoner. I don't know how I knew, but the knowledge cascaded over me like a shower of ice water. These men were making very certain that I did not get away from them.

And I remembered when and where I had seen that Berber's face. He had ridden in the caravan! He had paused in his flight to try a shot at me and had then lost his nerve.

These were riders of the Black Sultan!

Abu 'l Hasan would want me, quite naturally. I had killed two of his captains in the space of two seconds and had wiped out an excellent chance of murdering El Zidan.

I could only guess at what lay ahead, but I knew it as clearly as though it had been written on a wall in fire. Torture. Execution. My severed head in El Zidan's hands, sent triumphantly as a threat.

The two riders were watching my hands, but the darkness was thick. I could not turn about and ride back through the press of horses behind me. I could only dash straight ahead down this winding pass and take what lay in store at the far end.

El Zidan's automatics were solid against my thighs. I stretched casually, yawned and started to fumble in my breast pockets as though searching for a cigarette. My palms were hot and moist and I wondered if they'd stick to blue steel.

Abruptly I jerked the stallion's reins. He reared and his front feet struck wildly before him. My fingers lanced down to my belt and the automatics came out.

One of the Berbers shrieked a warning. They closed in about me like a pack of wild dogs, only holding their fire because they might hit their fellows. I fired without aiming at the grey ghosts about me.

The stallion hit the ground running. Every tendon was a tight wire, putting speed into our flight. Hoofs hammered. Steel struck fire from flinty stones. Powder flame lit up the pass like a flickering torch.

Crouching low over the pommel I raced down the defile, the cold night air clammy and hard against my face. The satiny djellaba cracked out from my shoulders and stood straight away from me, held back by the wind. My boots gripped the saddle.

It was like running through a black box with a treadmill floor.

I could not see the cliffsides, but the stallion sensed them. I expected any instant to plunge into nauseating space. I expected to feel the numbing shock of a bullet in my spine. I expected to feel the Arabian's staunch legs buckle under him.

But the djellaba cracked like a wind-whipped flag and the steel-shod hoofs rattled on the packed dirt like snare drums.

A glow against the low sky ahead. Perhaps the reflection of many fires. Perhaps—the thought dazed me—perhaps I was hammering straight toward the Black City!

No place to turn, no time to think. Behind me came the muttering of many hoofs. On either side were the hemming walls. No more shots now, and I thought I knew why. They were certain of me and a Berber does not waste expensive ammunition. Yes, they were certain of me and I was rocketing onward into their trap.

The path went down and the stallion buck jumped, all four feet braced against the steepness of the trail. Between the flat silhouette of his ears I saw a fresco done in ebony, sullen and shining and dangerous.

The Black City was spread out before me like a hand of cards. Lights threw sparks toward the dark sky. Minarets pointed ebon fingers at the stars. Rolling domes were massed like onyx marbles.

The gate was a tremendous affair of wrought iron, arched and open. Guards were there, white against black. They saw me charging them and they drew shoulder to shoulder, blocking my way. The stallion plunged toward the entrance. Carried by not-to-be-denied momentum, he was unable to stop.

By the glare of torches they could see the bunching, rippling muscles of his white chest.

Scimitars flashed, held ready. A long flintlock sprayed flame toward us. The Arabian catapulted toward the guards. Like flitting ghosts they scattered.

Pavement was under the stallion's feet. Black pavement shining as though polished by rain. Yellow windows were on either side, filled with shouting men. Spurring ahead I wondered if I could find another gate on the other side.

In the exact center of the city rose a mammoth pile of black masonry, dominating the houses about it. Towers, abutments, battlements, clung together to make an imposing whole.

I reined in and stared at it. This must be the Black Sultan's palace!

The decision was made in the flicker of an eye. I roweled the stallion and we hammered toward the palace, wind buffeting us. A wide high column of steps lay before us, curving upward.

The Arabian took the flight in powerful strides. At the top a Sudanese in a black robe uncoiled himself and stared down at us. Arms loose, shoulders hunched, his scimitar glittered.

El Zidan's right automatic rapped and the Sudanese stumbled and rolled past us, striking each separate step. We plunged through the arched doorway and clattered down another flight.

Smooth, polished boards were underfoot, shiny in the light of smoking torches. The stallion's steel-shod hoofs thundered across the outer courtroom.

A wide doorway to the left was inviting. We hammered toward it. A sea of silk met my eyes. Faces and veils. Sleek white bodies. I heard the wail of a pipe cut off short. A dead silence dropped, touched only by the hiss of a fountain.

I was as alarmed as the people before me. I had entered the palace harem!

One pair of eyes, infinitely blue, were regarding me with hot intensity. It was the girl of the caravan, unveiled. In that space of time, less than two heartbeats, I returned her gaze.

Then I spurred forward across the brilliant room. The stallion cleared the railing at the far end and then plunged through another door.

A high-ceilinged hall of awesome proportions was before me.

Hundreds of candles burned in the high, jeweled chandelier. Black columns stood half in light, half in shadow.

At the far end, seated upon a raised platform, a man sat cross-legged, surrounded by a score of glittering attendants.

The stallion had not stopped. I jabbed the spurs into his lathered flanks and jerked the reins. He halted in the center of the floor and reared. His hoofs pawed at the air, steel shoes sparkling in the light.

Clinging to his almost vertical back, I managed a salute. The staring eyes of the men before me widened.

In French, I said, "I have come to call upon the Black Sultan!"

The Arabian settled easily back. His forefeet clanged on the polished boards. The silk robe floated down about my shoulders and the automatics flashed in the candlelight.

"Who are you?" The man on the raised platform cried out.

"Your guest," I replied.

The courtiers shifted uneasily, fingering belted guns. From without came the insistent roar of a mob. Though I tried not to show it in my face, I was ripped apart by anxiety.

It would be easy for this Black Sultan to break the Mohammedan dictates of hospitality. If he bided by them he would have to give me my three days' food and lodging, if not he had only to raise his hand to the men about him and lead would stream from a dozen muzzles to cut me down.

The Black Sultan stood up, tall, thick of body, his beard pointed, his eyes as unreadable as a vulture's. His dark cloak swirled as he stepped easily forward.

The staring eyes of the men before me widened.
In French, I said, "I have come to call upon the Black Sultan!"

I knew then that he was without fear. He could see the flashing butts of my guns. He knew that I could fire before he could raise his voice or dodge. And yet he walked toward me with a slow stride and pinned me with his gaze.

The only sounds in that room were the gusty breathing of the Arabian, and the pad of the Black Sultan's slippers. The black plume which topped his black turban bobbed gracefully. His pointed face was expressionless. His thin jaw was steady. His djellaba swirled from side to side like a slowly drifting thundercloud.

One word from him and I would be pitched to the hardwood floor, riddled. I wondered who I would take with me. The Black Sultan first, the man in the red slippers second, the—I probably would live no longer than that.

The stallion shifted nervously. His ears went up as he watched the Black Sultan come toward us. And then the man was there, staring up into my face.

"An American," he said without emotion. "And a man with steel nerves. I thought at first that you were the mad El Zidan."

I had no answer for him, though his pause was long.

At last he turned toward the men about the platform.

"Stable this horse and show this man to a set of fine rooms." He spoke in Arabic, not Shilha. "Give him what he wants, anything he wants, for three days. But take his guns."

He looked back up to me with his lazy, hard glance and smiled.

"After three days, we will take you to the city gates and shoot you down as you strive to make the pass."

CHAPTER FOUR

The Girl at the Window

THE Black City had become a repulsive sight to me by
the end of the third day. There was a certain gagging
sullenness about the way the ebon buildings were crowded
together which wore on my nerves. The window was too high
for me to hear the street noises and so I lived in a silent void
enlivened only by the regular change of the guard outside my
door.

The walls of my room were painted in murals, hidden in
places by huge silken drapes which hung down to the floor.
It must have suited the Black Sultan's mood to have me so
well housed and fed, giving me, rather sarcastically, the three
days of hospitality required by the Koran.

Stepping off the length of the room for the thousandth
time I heard the door open. I had expected to see another
Sudanese or Berber. Another pair of curve-toed slippers and
a turban. But not an olive drab wool shirt, a pair of run-over
lace boots and a briar pipe.

The stranger stood with his back to the closed door, lounging
against it, studying me through a vile-smelling cloud of blue
smoke.

His eyebrows looked like thatched hut roofs and his nose
lay flatly against his right cheek. What remained of his hair
was sandy gray. His skin was a polished red.

31

"I been wondering what you looked like," he stated, burring his "r"s. "They told me you was an Englishman, but you ain't English. That's why I didn't come sooner. I thought you was English. I'm Scotch, myself."

He nodded and dragged on his pipe. The gurgling in-draft was loud in the room. "I'm McKenna. I handle Hasan's horses—them as El Zidan hasn't stole." He removed the pipe and sighed deeply. "There's no use in your trying to outride Hasan's bullets," he continued. "It can't be done."

"Can't outride them?"

"No, there's two kasbahs on either side of the trail as you come down the pass. You probably didn't see them. But those two forts are plenty to protect the Black City. Last fellow that tried to outride Hasan's bullets almost made it, and then, when he thought he was out of range, he plunked straight into the forts and they dropped him as slick as anything."

"Who was he?"

"I forget. A Spaniard I suppose. Hasan's got a grudge against Spaniards. You see, laddie, Hasan makes his own ammunition. Soft-nosed slugs. I've seen one of them tear the heart right out of a man. Once, down on the coast, I saw a feller's head blown off with just one shot. Terrible things, these dum-dums. Inhuman!"

I watched the smoke roll out of his pipe bowl and leaned back into the cushions.

"In the morning," he said, "you're going to get it. I can't help you out, so don't ask me. I thought you was English, but I see you're American, and even that don't alter the case.

However—" He paused, his rheumy eyes wandering, avoiding mine. His right hand flexed as though the palm itched.

"Go on," I said.

"I thought maybe you'd like to get a letter out to somebody. And if you did, then I could take it for you. You could tell them you was about to kick off. I—I'd only ask a hundred dollars or so. Maybe it would be worth that to you—now."

I stood up so suddenly that he dodged, though I had no intention of hitting him.

"McKenna, there's nothing I'd like better than to give you a hundred dollars. In fact, I'd like to see you get all the money I've got."

"Say, laddie, that's mighty—"

"On one condition!"

His watery eyes went shifty. He cleared his throat, drooping.

"That you put me in touch with a certain girl here who has gold hair and blue eyes."

"The—the redhead? My God, laddie, the Sultan is about to marry her! It's as much as my life is worth—"

I reached into my pocket and drew forth a stack of franc notes. The Sultan had not seen fit to rob me—not yet.

McKenna licked his lips, muttering to himself. Then he reached out for the money. I put it back in my pocket.

"After the girl is here," I said definitely.

"I'll—I'll see what I can do," he stammered, clicking the door shut behind him.

The yellow moon was coming up above the shaggy mountains. A pool of light lay in the center of the polished floor. For the next half-hour I paced nervously up and down, carefully stepping over the patch of yellow which lay in the shape of the arched window.

Suddenly I was aware of a change in the room. Still deep in thought, I was staring at the glowing floor pattern.

A shadow lay across it!

The girl was sitting on the window ledge, in profile to me, knees drawn up. She was dressed in filmy, translucent material which limned her in a gossamer froth of white. For seconds I stood staring at her silhouette. Her tinkling bracelets brought me back.

Her voice, soft and husky, barely reached me.

"You wanted to see me?"

I had, but now that she was here, I did not know why. I had nothing to say to her. In my hard, tempestuous career I had little room left for the chivalrous thing. I couldn't sweep into a graceful bow and tell her that I was her white knight, come to steal her away.

"You are British?" she said.

My lost voice came back:

"American. Eddie Moran is my name. Late of French Indochina, late of northern Morocco, and soon to be the *late* Eddie Moran."

"I know,"—soft and husky, barely reaching me.

"Who are you?" I asked her.

"My name is Sheila Gordon. Months ago I was stolen by Hasan's men in Fez. Shortly, I am to marry him."

Her bracelets tinkled again and I thought of Japanese wind

chimes in a garden on a summer night. I heard myself say, "Don't worry. I'll get you out of this."

She turned and shook her head.

"Don't offer me hope. You're a dead—" Her wristlets rang sharply as she realized what she was saying.

"Where is McKenna?"

"On the next floor. He let me down to the grille with his hands."

Leaning out, I whistled for the Scotchman.

"McKenna, here's your chance!"

His head appeared against the sky above me.

"McKenna, I've got a job for you. How would you like to earn five thousand dollars in gold?"

His scowl was softened by the moonlight, but it was still a scowl.

"How am I to earn that?"

"My friend, Godfrey Harrison, the vice-consul, will pay you if you deliver Sheila Gordon into his hands." It was a wild, mad shot in the dark. "Harrison has plenty of money and so have I. You could garb the girl in a man's clothes, get a couple of horses from your stable and ride away. Just a two weeks' ride, McKenna, for five thousand dollars."

"How do I know I'll get it?"

"McKenna," I said. "Did you ever hear of Rockefeller in the United States?"

"Sure."

"Well, I'm Rockefeller's favorite nephew."

"No!" he said, amazed.

35

"Yes, that's right. Just take the girl and—"

"Stop talking!" He hissed back. "I'll do it, even if she is English."

When I stepped back into the room, Sheila Gordon touched my arm.

"Do you think—?"

"Certainly I do. You'll get through all right, if you ride fast. McKenna has charge of the Sultan's horses and it ought to be easy. Here, I'll write a note to Harrison."

I fished through my pockets and found a pencil. Tearing a piece of white silk from a drape I wrote:

> Dear Harrison:
>
> IOU five thousand dollars. Collect from my insurance if it hasn't lapsed.
>
> Eddie Moran

It was fairly legible, even by moonlight. I gave it to her and she thrust it under her tightest bracelet. Standing close to me she looked up into my face.

"How can I ever— I can't leave you to die!"

"You can pay me," I told her. "Easily."

Before she could avoid my arm I swept her in close to me, crushing her against me. For one giddy second I kissed her. Then, a little dazed, I swung her into my arms, carried her to the window and handed her through and up.

McKenna's hands gripped hers.

Her soft husky voice floated down to me:

"Goodbye, Eddie Moran."

CHAPTER FIVE

The Palace Garden

I forgot to pace the room. I sank down on a pile of cushions facing the window and cupped my chin in my hands, staring at the spot where I had seen her last. Odd how that husky voice still lingered! Lingered as did the errant whispers of her perfume.

She had been a perfect painting, sitting there in profile on the broad sill. I began to wish that I had been able to paint. A painter was lucky. He could capture the things which pleased him, imprison them and look at them whenever the fancy took him.

A soldier could only remember and sit and wait for the moon to be drowned in sunlight. Perhaps I wouldn't be waiting for that if I had had talent in other directions. If I had been a Leonardo Da Vinci, for instance—

Thought flowed on, incoherent, tangled. Impressions came back and shimmered briefly before my eyes only to be crowded away by other impressions.

But something about Leonardo stayed with me. He had been a versatile fellow. He had written long papers on any and every subject. He had even forecast planes and the fact that man could fly.

He had even drawn a picture of a parachute—

Parachute!

Blinking I kept looking at the window, wondering if it could be possible, if I could get away with it.

Parachute!

How simple it would be to drop out and to the ground, floating through that barring space on silken wings!

Restlessly I went to the arch and looked down. It was a long drop, ended by uncompromising stone. Something about height always makes me a little sick in my midriff. In a plane I don't mind it at all—there isn't any connecting link to the ground. But height connected by a building side—

The draperies against the wall hung listlessly. I had torn one. Fingering the light silk, I felt resolve flood through me. I jerked the cloth down and discovered that it was about twelve feet by twenty-five feet.

What had Leonardo Da Vinci said? Twenty feet square to support a man? Thirty feet? Thirty-four feet?

I ripped another drape from the wall and flung it out beside the first. Looking hastily around the room I spotted a loosely woven rug. With unsteady fingers I unraveled it.

Taking the diamond clasp from the turban cloth I detached the pin and saw that it had a hole in the end for its hinge.

Using the rug thread and the pin needle I made short work of joining the two great wall coverings. The stitching was far from regular but I hoped it would hold.

My hands were shaking with excitement as I started to gather in the ends of the cloth to complete the task. And then I went as cold and stiff as an ice statue.

Men were coming down the outer hall to my room!

No time to gather up the silk. No time to hide my work. The door was flung open and the Black Sultan stamped into the chamber, his black eyes as hot as cinders.

"Search this place!" He roared at his courtiers.

They scattered out, flinging the draperies aside, kicking the piles of cushions. I sat calmly down and watched them.

Abu 'l Hasan turned on me.

"You have seen her?" he demanded.

"Who?" I inquired as innocently as possible.

"The English girl! The guard stated he heard her voice coming from this room and now she cannot be found. If this be true, American—"

He caught sight of the silk, then, and stopped, frowning. His black djellaba twitched angrily as he came nearer.

I shoved my hands into my pockets and smiled.

"It is customary in our country to make a shroud for the dead," I told him. "Knowing your customs, I thought I had better make my own."

The pointed black beard was jutting.

"Then you know the folly of trying to outride my rifles. A shroud, eh?" Something in the word made him laugh. The sound was like a saw going through hard wood. I did not know whether or not he believed me. I was certain he could hear my heart bang against my ribs.

He turned to the door and flung up his arm for his men to follow him. When the door banged shut I heard him say, "Chicken-livered fool! A shroud! That is—"

I sat calmly down and watched them.

I flung myself upon the silk and gathered up the four ends. By fastening the unraveled thread to the edges and corners I made a fairly presentable harness.

The thing dragged out behind me as I stepped up on the sill. The black emptiness of space was below me. I wondered how I could ever summon enough nerve to make the jump. If this thing should happen to catch on the building as I went down—if the threads should rip out—if it failed to open at all—

A strong wind was coming down from the hills, blowing past the tower. I counted upon it to help me. It was better than outriding rifles anyway. I'd get it over with. I tossed the wad of cloth before me. The wind snapped at it.

It was open, and my fingers on the ledge were slipping. When I could hold on no longer, I let go.

I swooped downward and out like a pendulum. The chute jerked and dropped fifty feet in the breadth of a second. I swung back.

The side wall crashed into me, dazing me. The chute was fighting to get loose. I felt a thread snap, another, and still another. For harrowing moments I was certain that I would fall free to the waiting pavement.

But before I had time to worry about it, I was down. I slid out of my harness and the silk went slapping away into the gloom, carried by the wind.

I knew that I was far from free but I was at least out of the tower. Unarmed, in a wall city I did not know, and without a horse.

From under my belt I pulled the djellaba and turban, putting them on. They at least made me a little less conspicuous, even though their color was clearly distinguishable in the night.

I slid along a wall, studying my surroundings, holding the restless cloak tight to my body. If I could just find my way to the gate—

A wall was against me and I turned to follow it. It squared off and traveled at right angles. Ten seconds later I knew that fate was giving me a raw deal. I had dropped into a palace garden, not into a street! I could thank the wind for that.

An arched entrance was a luminous patch in the gray wall. In the moonlight I could see steps rising up to it. This would lead into the palace, but I couldn't hope to scale the barriers of the garden and there seemed to be no other exit.

Putting on the boldest front possible, I strode up the steps, heels ringing, cape flowing out behind me. The hall was long, high-ceilinged and narrow. Smoking torches burned in the niches, throwing jumpy shadows against the stone.

A Sudanese guard was leaning against a column at the far end, rifle barrel loosely held in his black fist. He heard me come and turned. I could see the flash of white eyeballs against the black face.

Because I did not falter, he did not take alarm. He merely stood there and watched me come. A cigarette sent a spiral of smoke up his side to eddy about his white-turbaned head.

It was not until I was within five feet of him that he knew something was wrong. I hoped that his religion was good, that he had been prompt in his *salāt,* his cleansing *wudu'* and that he would get his forty damsels in heaven.

His teeth flashed. He jumped back and swung up the gun. But he had waited too long; and when one has taught and used the rifle in all of its various forms—

Gripping the muzzle, I flung it straight back. The steel-shod butt crashed into his chest. Wrenching the gun from him I reversed it and smashed his skull. He had not had time to pull the trigger, nor to shout. Slumping to the base of the column, his hands relaxed and fell into his lap. A casual observer would have said that he slept.

I took his djellaba and threw it over my own, pulling up the oversize hood to cover my red turban and to hide my face. Tossing the rifle over the crook of my arm I walked across the hardwood floor.

After I had crossed three rooms, I knew that I was hopelessly lost. There were too many which looked too much alike. I could find no doors which led to the outside.

A fountain was tinkling somewhere ahead and I made my way toward it. The room was of mighty proportions, all in black. A staircase led upward— I recognized the outer hall of the palace which I had entered upon the Arabian.

I had started toward the steps when the sound of voices came to me. A door creaked weightily upon its hinges and the words became distinct. The voice of the Black Sultan was saying:

"Can't really rely upon the patrols to pick them up. They'll be miles away by morning."

A mutter of agreement followed.

Hasan's voice was tight with repressed anger, held in check only by effort.

"Get the white stallion and cavalry: Bring them to the door. Go quickly. We will give chase."

Men entered the outer hall. It was useless to try to make the stairs. I pressed myself back into the shadows and brought the rifle up to present arms.

Without a glance the Black Sultan's officers passed within a yard of me. They were too used to seeing sentries at odd places in the palace.

When they had disappeared, I started in their wake and then stopped. After all I had no horse and no way to get free. I might as well talk to Hasan before I left.

I went back to the throne room and kicked the door open. The black columns and sparkling candles were mirrored in the black, polished floor. Hasan, in his dark cloak, paced nervously before his throne. He looked up angrily and I entered.

The soldier's djellaba slipped away from me. I stood with my boots apart, rifle centered on his chest.

He loosed a startled gasp and raised his head to call.

"I wouldn't," I said. "I ask nothing more than an excuse to murder you."

El Zidan's two glittering automatics were swinging from Hasan's waist but he did not try for them. He was a brave man but he knew suicide when it appeared stark before him.

"The English girl," I said, "is miles from here by now. You can't catch up with her. As a matter of fact, Hasan, I don't believe you'll ever see her again."

"Why?"

"Because I'm going to kill you."

He stumbled back against the platform, supporting himself with his hands on the edge. "What have I—" He realized that what he was about to say would sound foolish. "Moran, I'll pay you well, I'll let you go free."

"I believe you," I replied. "Implicitly. If you want to save yourself another minute of existence, unbuckle your cartridge belts, let your guns drop to the floor and take off your cloak."

The automatics and holsters slithered about his boots, the djellaba fluttered down. He edged slowly toward the far end of the platform. I had no real wish to shoot him. Whatever else I may be, I'm not a coldblooded murderer.

He started to speak again:

"Gold, Moran, would buy you much while my life would only buy you torture. I am—"

Footsteps and a sharp intake of breath were behind me. I whirled about and saw that a captain had come back. He opened his mouth to shout, and grabbed at his waistline.

I threw the rifle like an athlete's hammer. The butt cracked as it struck his face. He sank down with a moan, holding his head, blood leaking through his quivering fingers.

Turning, I saw that the Black Sultan was gone. I scooped the automatics up from the floor and buckled them about me. I flung Hasan's djellaba over my own and affixed the hood. It might serve my purpose for five minutes or so.

Trying to keep from running, I went through the room of the fountain and walked up the steps. The night air was cold against my cheeks. The moon was directly overhead, throwing my face into shadow.

At the bottom of the outer stairs stood a group of horsemen.

White and shining among them was the Arabian stallion. I descended, slowly, thrusting aside hands which reached out to help me. It was hard to swing up into the saddle without exposing the fact that I wore a white cloak beneath the black, but when faced with eternity a man can contrive almost anything.

They had not looked closely at me. Their eyes were respectfully gazing into the distance. I waved my hand and guided the Arabian ahead.

With two officers in the vanguard we rode out toward the gates of the city. The stallion was rested and ready for anything. It required a strong hand to hold him in. His walk was as smooth as flowing oil.

The rhythmic clatter of many hoofs was sharp in the cold night air. The moonlight was more blue than white. The mountains were mighty slabs of black cardboard, ragged against the sky.

Guns in present arms at the gate, the kasbahs and the pass ahead. Grey ghosts stalking beside me, guarding the cloak of their ruler, hoping to return by morning, in time to witness the execution of a certain American who had killed two of their officers.

I was riding with death at my stirrups.

CHAPTER SIX

Machine-Gun Business

IN the deep shadow of the pass, cut off from the direct rays of the moon, we picked our way among the boulders. The two officers in the lead rode stiffly and those on either side of me glanced neither to the right nor left—riding like so many marionettes on puppet mounts.

For hours we went on, wordless, intent only upon the defile. My nerves were growing steadily tighter, until I finally felt that I would have to yell or throw things or shoot or ride hell for saddle away from them.

I almost welcomed the sounds of the approaching horseman. The Sultan's troopers drew in and sat, waiting, hands on guns. They reminded me of vultures crouched on a rail fence.

The lone horse was coming slowly as though tired. Rocks rolled under the shuffling hoofs. I strained my eyes through the gloom and at last I saw the rider.

It was McKenna!

The two officers ahead guided their mounts in alongside the Scotchman. With a startled exclamation, he stopped and looked at us. His hands were shaking on the reins; even in the blue moonlight I could see his face turn ashen.

He was so startled that he forgot to speak Shilha.

"What—what the hell are you—I mean—"

The officers turned to me. I put out my hand as though

47

shoving them away and rode in close to McKenna. One question was burning in my throat. Where was Sheila Gordon?

The Sultan's men seemed unwilling to draw away. My hand was insistent. For terrible seconds I thought they would force me to speak—and that would be the end.

Shoving my face close to McKenna's, I whispered:

"What happened to the girl?"

He jumped as though I had struck him. His horse shied. His eyes were light patches in the shadow of his face.

"*Moran!* How did—"

"Shut up!" I warned him. "They think I'm Hasan. What happened?"

"A bunch of men up the pass jumped us and I got away."

"And left her? A hell of a man *you* are. Listen. Talk for me. Tell me loud, in Shilha, that you and I had better go back and locate her."

He had recovered from his scare and he knew that in betraying me he would put his own neck in the cutting block. Loudly, he bawled out the truth of the matter, calling me Hasan.

I drew back and started up the pass. The Sultan's men seemed determined to follow.

"Tell them," I said to McKenna, "that I'm going on alone. Tell them to go back and gather up the troops in case anything happens to me."

McKenna wheeled his horse in the trail. His voice was like a foghorn.

"His Majesty says to go back! He says you make too much noise. Go gather up the troops and stand ready!"

I didn't breathe easily until we had placed a quarter of a mile between the soldiers and ourselves. Those men would probably return, marveling at the Sultan's bravery, but when they reached the Black City, they'd hear from Hasan and pursuit would come like a tornado.

McKenna, coaxing his tired mount into a faster trot, rode at my stirrup.

"Tell me. How in the devil did you—"

"Save it," I said. "It isn't important. How far along on this trail did you lose Sheila Gordon?"

"It's a half a night's ride," he whined. "You've got me in a terrible jam, Moran. I just remember that they'll know I'm with you and that I'm your friend. I can't go back; and I might have if—"

"You didn't have any chance to go back. If you'd opened your big mouth wrong down the trail I'd have blown you apart. I had a gun in your stomach all the time I was talking to you."

"You—you didn't!" His tone immediately changed. "Now listen, Moran, I'm a friend of yours, ain't I, now? You know how I tried to get you out of there, laddie. You know all the risk I took."

"Sure. I know. Now shut up and ride. If you can't keep up with me, that's your hard luck."

I turned the stallion loose. So far, the ride had just warmed him up and he was aching to run. His slender legs struck out and the pass fled away like a river of black oil.

For a while McKenna managed to keep within sight of me. He was in no real danger of dropping into the hands of the patrol which would undoubtedly follow and I let him fall behind. Besides there was only one trail and he couldn't get lost.

Sheila Gordon was my real worry. McKenna did not know anything about the men who had jumped them. Probably the same men would jump me. But if they did, I was certain that they would find the going rough.

The false dawn hung in the east when I first heard the sound. It was a ragged crackle ahead of me, not unlike the drumming of the stallion's hoofs. The noise became more distinct and I reined in, listening.

It was rifle fire!

Going on for another hundred yards I paused again. This time I could ascertain the types of rifles. The Lebel has a certain hollow bark which can be distinguished from any other shot. And Lebels in quantity should not, could not be in hands of tribesmen!

Something was definitely wrong with this. Lebels, punctuated by the occasional rap of Sniders. I could understand the Sniders, even the report of Mannlichers and flintlocks. But not Lebels. Certainly the French Foreign Legion had no business this high in the Atlas. Of course it was within their policing zone, but their reasons for being here were beyond me.

But Lebels meant Legion, and I was wanted by the French. It was foolhardy to go on. I turned the stallion, forgetting for an instant that Hasan would probably be hitting the trail about now, with flame in his eye. Forgetting that there was no escape from the long pass behind me.

Minutes ticked by and I still sat there, listening to the crescendo of rifle fire. It was certain that someone stood between me and the Legion. And that someone might treat me better than either the French or the Black Sultan.

I rode forward at a walk. Before I had gone fifty yards, two men sprang down into the trail ahead of me, throwing up their rifles. In the same instant I held up my hands, showing them that they were empty.

A face appeared over the top of a boulder. The cold yellow sunlight threw sparks from a diamond turban pin. A man of huge proportions stepped into the trail and strode toward me, his right hand outstretched and empty.

It was El Zidan!

My relief was so great that I started laughing, and though they could not see the point, the two sentries began to laugh with me. And El Zidan's roaring chuckle was added to the chorus.

"This," said El Zidan, his blue eyes twinkling, "is the best yet! All night last night I was wishing I could laugh. Now I feel better. Come along, Eddie Moran, we've a jammed machine gun up here that you can probably fix."

"Gladly," I replied. "What's happening on the front?"

"Oh, the French! They get such foolish ideas and do such silly things. But with all, they're amusing at times. They think we're trying to hit them."

"But why in the name of God should the French be here, after you?"

"Because of you, Eddie Moran. This Nicolle spoke hastily before I left town and I punished him. And now the French think I'm threatening the peace of Morocco."

"Certainly there's more to it than that!"

He offered me a cigarette and then spoke with one between his lips. "Yes, I suppose there is. Abu 'l Hasan has been spreading stories about me, and the French think Abu 'l Hasan is the greatest fellow that ever walked. They have to think that or they lose a good part of Morocco. And as Abu 'l Hasan doesn't like me— Well, it's really very simple, after all."

"Tell me. What did you do with the girl you stopped last night?" I tried to keep the interest out of my voice. After all, I wasn't quite sure of El Zidan on every score.

"Girl? What—oh, yes! I remember now. A rather pretty lady, isn't she? Sheila Gordon, she said her name was. Of course she might be Sheila Gordon, at that. Wait, Moran. Listen. How did you know I had her here?"

"Magic," I replied. "Is she all right?"

"Quite. I'll send her over to you when you get the gun fixed. We need the gun, you see. By the way, Moran, I'm not quite sure of where I am. Is this the long pass to the Black City?"

"It is. And there's no escape from it once you start going down."

"And the Black Sultan?"

"Is probably on his way right this minute to get Sheila Gordon and myself."

"Oh, I say!" El Zidan's blue eyes stopped twinkling. The cigarette dangled limply from his mouth. I would have laughed at that English phrase coming from such a thoroughly picturesque Berber had it not been for the calamitous expression on his face. I felt sorry for him, momentarily forgetting that I was in the same boat.

"How many men have you?" I demanded.

"About two hundred, I suppose."

"And how many Legionnaires are out there?"

"A battalion, probably. I haven't had time to count them."

He stood with his red-booted feet apart, his fingers hooked casually into his cartridge belts, his white silk djellaba flowing away to his silver-spurred heels. His thoughts were well hidden behind his strong face.

I loosened my guns in their holsters. "A battalion in front of you, Abu 'l Hasan rolling up behind with a thousand troopers, a pass on either side of you."

"That's right," he assented.

The soldier in me seized the upper hand. With some heat I demanded:

"Well, why in the name of the seven great devils did you let yourself get into such a position?"

"I—well, I had some hazy idea of pulling you out of the Black City."

He said it gently enough, but I felt as though I'd been hit in the face with a sledge hammer. In no little confusion, I muttered:

"Come on, let's do something about it."

I scrambled up over the rocks. When I reached the top of a ridge, he pulled me back in time to save me from getting my head blown off. The sniper's bullet yowled away down the pass.

"They mean business," I commented. "Where's the machine gun?"

He pointed to a barricade of stone and we crawled over to it. The gunner was sitting on his haunches nursing a wounded shoulder, gazing dejectedly at the Hotchkiss.

There was not a great deal wrong with it. They had let the gun get too hot—that was all. Oil, water and three minutes with a spanner did everything necessary. I felt that I could hold that spot now against a division.

CHAPTER SEVEN

One Slim Chance

TAWNY piles of boulders mounting to the metallic blue sky. Green valleys lost in distance. Cliffs rising sheerly, bearded by desperately clinging trees. A sun, climbing up to high noon and withering heat.

I did not try to hit anything with the Hotchkiss. I fired only to show them that the ravine was not to be crossed. But if they could not cross, then neither could we. They had us securely bottled in the mouth of the pass. I counted the passing hours and sweated over the knowledge that we would be crushed between the closing jaws of a bear trap.

A hand was on my shoulder, tugging at me. I rolled over on my side. Sheila Gordon smiled and pulled my fingers away from the gun trips.

"I didn't recognize you at first," she said. "You're all black with gun smoke."

I noted that she had begged a change of clothing. A white Berber shirt, a pair of Zouave trousers and red sandals had replaced the flimsy material she had worn when I first saw her. Her hair streamed down over her shoulders in a cascade of pure gold. She seemed more real, more approachable.

"If you don't like gun smoke, don't sit there."

She moved a little, out of the ejector's range. A bullet snapped at the barricade and she dodged. The hollow report of the shot reached us a fraction of a second after and she dodged a second time.

"You don't like it much, do you?"

"No. Why should I? It's all so silly. Those men out there haven't even met you. Don't know you at all!"

"Do you have to be formally introduced to a guy before you can kill him?"

"No. You understand what I mean. Those men aren't even Frenchmen. They're Legionnaires. And you people aren't rebels or anything like that. I don't quite catch on."

"They're fighting us because they think we're bad medicine," I explained. "And because they're supposed to keep peace in Morocco at any price, including war. And we're fighting them because we want to get the hell out of here before Hasan rides up behind us."

She had the startling white complexion of all redheads, but her face went a shade lighter at the mention of Hasan's name. "He's coming to—"

"To take you and me back. He'll hear this firing and he'll sum it up quickly enough. And if I'm not mistaken he'll have every trooper of the Black Kingdom with him. I'm telling you because I don't want you to be scared out of your wits and because— Well, because there won't be any time to talk after Hasan gets here."

"But, Eddie! He'll kill us!"

"No, he won't kill you, but he'll have an awful lot of fun with me."

"You don't think I'd allow myself to be taken back, do you?"

"Why not? Try to escape some other way."

"I couldn't. Honestly I couldn't. You don't know what it is, staying there a prisoner, waiting, waiting for him to arrange things."

A flash across the ravine caught my attention. A bit of blue was visible there. Suddenly the opposing cliff face was alive and swarming. The attack was starting in earnest.

Yelling to the riflemen of El Zidan, I started to hammer lead into the rocks at the base of the other cliff. I had my orders. I was not to kill any Legionnaires. What orders in the face of all this!

The green and red and flashing avalanche poured across the bottom. The men were shouting shrilly, pausing to fire as they came on. A native to my right threw up his hands and pitched off the edge, screaming as he fell.

The belt rattled through the machine gun. Bullets flayed the path before the Legionnaires, warning them not to cross all the way over.

I was instantly aware of a patch of color just under the muzzle of the gun. Suddenly a Legionnaire was clearing the edge. He came at me, teeth bared, rifle and bayonet ready to put an end to me.

And I couldn't kill him! Orders! And I couldn't desert the gun because of the men pouring up the hill at us. But desert the gun I must.

Springing up, I reached for his barrel. His black beard bristled. His chest was ribboned, attesting his bravery. Averting the needlelike point, I swung a fist at his chin. He dodged, trying to bring the rifle back to thrusting position. Effort made his eyes blaze. His teeth were bared like the white fangs of a wolf.

My fist connected suddenly. He dropped the rifle and slumped down. With a yell, I skidded him over the edge and sent him bumping down the slope, little the worse for the encounter.

I caught an impression of Nicolle waving an automatic amid the maze of moving color. I heard his whistle shrill out a command. I started the Hotchkiss again. I could have slaughtered them in their tracks, but I could not for the sake of El Zidan's orders.

They turned and ran back to their cliff. They did not know that the machine gun carefully avoided them. God, how much longer could we keep this sort of thing up?

For some minutes, things were quiet. The girl was starry-eyed behind me, scarcely breathing. She knew what we were up against.

I got busy with the gun. Two Legionnaires had crept down to the bottom of the trail. They went back with bullets rapping their heels.

The Hotchkiss stopped hammering and I saw that the belt was all the way through. "You are sitting on the cartridge cases," I said. "Please pass the belts."

She moved aside and glanced down. When her blue eyes came up to mine, I knew. But in that flickering second I didn't think of the calamity of being without ammunition. I marveled at how well we understood one another without speaking.

El Zidan came up and pulled at my boot. I turned and shook my head.

"All gone. Better get a couple of riflemen up here to cover this place."

"Can't spare any," he said.

"But they'll cross the ravine and flank us!"

"Can't help it," replied El Zidan. He sat back on his silver-spurred heel and lit a cigarette. When he had it going, he shifted it to the corner of his mouth and said:

"Unless you have any ideas, Moran, we're whipped. I'd rather surrender to the French than—"

"I've been getting ideas all morning," I said. "But none of them will work. If you surrender to the French, Hasan will use his influence to send you to jail for life. The tide's turned and it will stay that way."

"And the French will—" He made a motion across his throat with his index finger and then pointed at me.

I looked about me. The bare brown mountains were a mammoth prison, holding us. In all this great solemnity, rifles were like terriers barking in a cathedral. The sun was hot and dry against my back.

Sheila tossed her hair away from her face with a slender hand.

"Perhaps—if I were to give myself up to Hasan—"

"Stay the thought," said El Zidan. "Moran loves you."

Startled, she caught her breath and looked at me. Evidently the bald truth of the matter was disconcerting.

After a moment I sat up and looked back down the pass.

"What happened to McKenna?" I wondered.

"Who's McKenna?" asked El Zidan. "The man who just rode into camp?"

"So he got here finally! Maybe I have a use for McKenna." Sheila sniffed.

"He rode off and left me," she said. "I don't see what use he could be."

I shook my head. "You never can tell how a man will come in handy."

El Zidan took a long drag on his cigarette.

"What are you thinking of doing?"

"I don't know, exactly. The situation sizes up this way: with two hundred men, you can neither hold this position, nor battle your way out. And if we stay here we'll get squashed. Now listen, El Zidan, do you know this pass very well?"

"No. Hardly at all. I haven't even been down it since I was about so high. And then on my way out to England."

"How about Hasan?" I said. "He's a pretty conceited fellow. Do you think he's a military strategist?"

"I guess he is, the way we've played hide and seek."

"Then there's one slim chance that he'll fall for this. Sheila, you and I are the pawns. We lose most any way we look at it. You could go over to the French, but you can't unless we do. You're liable to get hurt staying here with us."

"Are you going to send me away?" she demanded.

"Yes, that's right." I stopped and thought the thing over. "And I'm sending myself away with you."

"Are you suffering from a *coup de soleil*?" cried El Zidan.

"No," I replied. "It's thumbs down on me and I'll take the

gamble where the odds are best. Sheila and I are going to ride down the trail and meet the Black Sultan."

"You're mad!" exclaimed El Zidan. "He'll kill you!"

"Not right away, he won't, and it's worth the risk. El Zidan, you promised to make me a grand vizier of the kingdom I'm going to hold you to that promise. Just so you'll keep it, I'm going to give you the kingdom."

"But it's certain death!" cried El Zidan.

"Any way you look at it. But I got you into this jam and I'll try to get you out."

Sheila was staring at me. She seemed convinced that I had lost my mind.

"Will you go?" I asked her.

"Anything you say is . . . is all right with . . . with me."

"Good girl! Let's go down and find McKenna. Duck low. Don't let those Frogs get a crack at your head."

We went sliding down the steep hill, and when we reached the horses, El Zidan laid his hand on my arm.

"Goodbye, Moran. I wish you luck. I can do that much. But—I know you won't come back."

CHAPTER EIGHT

Ready for the Slaughter

GRAND vizier of a kingdom! What a pitiful thought that was! El Zidan, bottled up in a pass, about to be hammered front and rear and obliterated. El Zidan's men, few and undergunned, about to run out of ammunition.

And I was galloping down the trail to meet Hasan and give myself up. I remember the way my torn silk sleeves whipped back, the way the djellaba cracked, the way the Arabian thundered onward, untiring.

Grand vizier of a kingdom! But then men will dream and plan and forget that there is, after all, some kind of proportion in life.

Sheila Gordon rode at my stirrup, her gold hair flowing back, the white collar of her Berber shirt whipping against her white cheeks, her blue eyes alight, reflecting my own determination.

Behind us, mounted on a fresh horse, came McKenna in his wool OD shirt and his greasy pants. He knew I was crazy, but he rode with me in the hope that he could thereby pull his own neck out of the fire.

El Zidan had his orders and if everything clicked off there was some scant hope. I wasn't remembering that even if I escaped Hasan, there were still the French.

Far ahead of us I caught sight of sun on a lance. I drew in and stopped McKenna.

"This," I said, "is where the farce begins. Give me your revolver."

He handed the ugly thing over and I flipped out the cylinder, pouring the glinting shells into the dirt. I gave it back to him.

Then I unwound my scarlet turban cloth and handed it to Sheila.

"Wrap my djellaba tight about me and then bind my arms with this cloth."

"But you'll be helpless!" she cried.

I pulled the two jeweled automatics from their holsters and gripped them, folding my arms across my chest.

"Not quite," I said. "I can shoot through a djellaba with surprising accuracy, and though you won't be able to see the guns, they'll be there. Tie away."

She wrapped the red turban cloth about my biceps and tied it. To all effect I was unarmed and helplessly bound.

"Remember," I said to McKenna, "these guns are ready to let go and if you happen to make the wrong move, you get it first, even before I shoot the Black Sultan."

His shaggy brows drew in close and he stared down at his empty gun. "But what'd you do this for?"

"You're the victor," I said. "You captured us and you're bringing us back to the Black Sultan to reinstate yourself. You tell him that much, but don't mention that El Zidan is at the other end of this pass—and don't contradict anything I say. If you're thinking of anything as brash as that, you'd better begin your prayers, if you know any."

"I'm a good churchman," he protested.

"Then ride on."

With the girl and myself in the lead, we rode at a walk toward the oncoming columns.

Hasan's soldiers rode double file, pennons fluttering, bright lances flashing, a martial study in black and white. They filled the pass back out of sight, and at their head came Hasan astride a nervous black horse.

When they sighted us, Hasan held up his hand and stopped.

McKenna had the empty gun trained on my back and I saw by his watery eyes that he was weighing his chances of getting away from the hidden muzzles.

Hasan's sharp face and vulture eyes betrayed no surprise. Hands resting on his pommel he waited for us to come within speaking distance. Sunbeams shattered themselves against a drawn revolver in an officer's hand.

McKenna laughed uneasily.

"I got them, Your Majesty. I waited until Moran was off his guard and I jumped him."

Hasan said nothing.

McKenna laughed again, uncertainly. "I brought them back to you, you see. That's what I had in mind all the time, Your Majesty."

The Black Sultan looked at me and then at the girl. His glance came back to my face.

"Why did you allow yourself to be taken?"

"Any man that trusts another deserves to get it in the neck," I said as bitterly as I could.

"You mean McKenna?" said Hasan.

"No, I mean El Zidan. He's a treacherous devil."

The Black Sultan leaned forward.

"You have seen El Zidan?" he demanded.

I spat deliberately.

"El Zidan is trying to attack you! He met with one of your patrols at the mouth of the pass."

"I have no report of this," said Hasan.

"They've been too busy to send reports. El Zidan has captured a French train and uniformed his men as Legionnaires, thinking you would admit them to the city before you knew who they were. He has machine guns aplenty!"

"You mean El Zidan is at the head of this pass?"

I nodded quickly. "He has many men, well armed, and as soon as he breaks through he'll pour down this gorge and wipe you out."

Hasan's eyes were wide, surprised and thoughtful at the same time.

"But then I must reinforce my patrol—"

"Yes," I jeered. "Reinforce your patrol. I always knew you were a weak-brained fool, Hasan. All might and no wits. I don't care what happens to El Zidan after what he did to me. I thought you wanted to take him prisoner."

"That's right," said Hasan, taking the bait. "I do want him prisoner. Then—then that means if I attack him from the rear, I'll be able—"

"Marvelous!" I said. "Simply marvelous! But you can't get out of this pass in time to do it. Did you leave a guard at your forts?"

66

"Why, of course I did."

"Then why don't you drive El Zidan down this pass and up against the walls of the city and wipe him out right there in your own front yard? Or haven't you the nerve to try that?"

"I can get out of this pass!" bellowed Hasan. "You think I would have something like this if I could not escape from it myself?"

"I'm amazed."

The Black Sultan wheeled his horse and pointed his finger at an officer.

"Locate the masked staircase I caused to be made. We shall ride over the ridge, get behind El Zidan and drive him down here and to his death.

"Si Alush, come here! Take this American and this girl back to the city and hold them there. Tell Umzien at the forts to make his machine guns ready for the slaughter. Tell him that his targets will be uniformed as Legionnaires.

"Ali! Ride forward alone along this trail until you contact our patrol. Tell them to fall back with all haste!"

Ali galloped forward toward El Zidan. Sentries would take care of him.

The column behind began to move. For a half-hour we trotted in their dust, unable to see what was taking place before us. And then the dry fog began to thin and I looked up startled to behold column after column riding along the ridge above us. They were gone from the pass.

The steps had been carved from rock, disguised by underbrush. Hasan was, after all, a military strategist. I had not supposed he would leave so long a pass without an exit for himself. Passes are apt to be embarrassing when they are too confining.

Si Alush rode beside McKenna, behind us, balancing a Snider across his pommel. His face was as hard as his diamond eyes and his fingers were thin and scaly on the trigger.

I looked back and saw the long lines of riders, black silhouettes against the metallic blue sky. They were disappearing on the other side of the ridge, striking out in a circle which would bring them into position behind Nicolle and his Legionnaires.

I laughed aloud, and Si Alush stared at me suspiciously. By this time El Zidan would be talking to Nicolle under a flag of truce and Nicolle would be using the lull to better his own position by crossing the ravine.

El Zidan would probably be discussing the weather or asking Nicolle for a cigarette and Nicolle would be threshing his tan boots with his riding crop, unable to understand why a flag of truce had been offered at all.

But I had little time to worry about that. I had my own work to do, and by the looks of Si Alush's eyes, the going would be hard.

CHAPTER NINE

Death at the Pass

IT was night when we reached the kasbahs at the head of the pass. Stars as bright as arc lights hung close to us from the sky. The shadowy mountains loomed about us, closer in the darkness. The moon was striving to rise above the horizon, casting a yellow glow between two mountains which stood together, leaving a gunsight between them.

The Black City was before us and below us, sullen and depressing with its ebon minarets and onyx domes.

We had come slowly enough, and with each passing minute my nerves had been tightened like the pegged strings on a banjo. The time element was too hard to gauge and if anything went wrong a number of good men would die and Sheila would be back with Hasan, and I would be shrouded by the white dust of the lime pit.

Odd how El Zidan had placed his confidence in me. He knew the chances against success even better than I. He had a better understanding of Imaziren vengeance. And when a Berber sets himself to square a score, he has a certain bitter humor which is not nice to contemplate.

The Black Sultan, if anything went wrong, would be far from mild in the treatment of both El Zidan and myself.

Si Alush stopped before the barred door of the squat stone fort and called out:

"Open up! I have orders from the Black Sultan!"

With a doleful creak, the heavy oak swung back, letting out a rectangle of light which left half of Si Alush in a shadow. I began to have misgivings.

After all, these two forts were placed in advantageous spots. They could command the entire pass entrance with their guns. I didn't want El Zidan to run into a horizontal leaden sleet.

Not even Nicolle and his Legionnaires deserved that.

It was up to me to force the issue. The stallion had done things like this before and he would have to do them again—now! "Untie the turban!" I whispered to Sheila.

Her fingers were swift, but Si Alush had been waiting for just that move. He whirled. The Snider was a black shadow against the yellow light. I fired through the djellaba.

Si Alush straightened as though he had been pulled up by a string. The Snider sagged slowly. And then it was as though the string had been abruptly severed. He crashed to the ground.

"Allah—illahu!" squealed a man in the fort.

I had clips for the automatic. Its moist grip felt competent in my hand. I had clips. And I had the incentive of knowing I either had to do this thing or die.

I rammed the spurs into the stallion's flanks. The sentry at the gate leaped at me. I fired straight into his face and plunged for the stairs.

The flight was not long. At the top the tower room glowed under the light of smoking torches. It was hazy up there, blurred with the bodies of hastily moving men. The machine guns were along the walls, pointing out at the pass.

As I went up I saw a Berber grab the tripod of a Browning.

He tried to swing the thing around, tried to shoot me as I came up. I shot from the waist as I rode. He died across the barrel.

There were six men in that room. For armament they had four machine guns. For close combat they had scimitars.

Faces distorted, they rushed toward the head of the stairs, trying to prevent my entrance into the guardroom. I fired as fast as I could pull the trigger. A huge, white-turbaned man, evidently an officer, fired at me with his revolver. In the same second I reached the room.

"*Ifrīt!*" they roared. "*Jinnī!* Devil!"

The officer, close beside me, fired again. Hot sticky fluid was coursing down my side, running into my boot. The room was spinning. I held hard to the pommel as the stallion reared.

Three men were still on their feet. They tried for the bridle. His steel-shod hoofs struck again and again. Then there were only two.

Seconds were hours. I had not been a full minute on my way. The .45 was still spitting flame although I did it through no actual will of my own. I was slipping from the saddle.

The officer, dragging me down, tried to beat at me with the gun. The .45 exploded close against his chest. My nostrils were filled with the reek of burning cloth. He pitched back, carrying me with him. His body broke my fall.

I lay there for seconds, expecting to be killed by a sword, too weak to do anything about it. Ironic fate. The man who had first tugged at the Browning was also under me, beside the captain. His machine gun was there, but I didn't seem to have will enough to reach it.

"El Zidan is coming!" cried Sheila from the stairs.

El Zidan. God, I had to do something! It gave me strength. I rolled over on my side. Relief flooded in upon me. The stallion and myself were the only living beings in that smoke-blued room.

And then I knew I was wrong. From another part of the tower I heard running feet. More men were coming. Even as I realized it I saw a djellaba and a scimitar enter. Only those two. I couldn't quite see the man though I could clearly see the flash of light from that steel.

I tried to do something, anything. I had to get free for the sake of El Zidan. The sword was close to me now, about to descend. And I was too weak to move!

Sheila Gordon's clear tones came up the stairs:

"El Zidan is coming!"

It was too late to do anything now, I thought. In the time it took the tempered steel to come down I found space enough to realize what would happen to El Zidan and Nicolle. The fort on the other side would take care of them.

"El Zidan is coming!" cried Sheila again.

It gave me strength, the sound of her voice. The cold snout of the machine gun was against my side. I rolled quickly over. The scimitar threw sparks as it struck the stone.

Before the clang had died away I had the machine gun in my hands. With a quick flip I set its tripod. The sultan's men were coming at me from across the room.

I thanked the gods that they had momentarily failed to spot me in the dim yellow light. Above me a torch was sputtering and smoking, throwing gigantic shadows behind the advancing Imaziren.

The machine gun let loose. My fingers wouldn't stick to the bloodgreased triggers. I was dizzy and somewhat short of breath. The ribbons of flame which fanned out away from me were dragon tongues.

Smoke drifted across the room, separating me from the Imaziren. The machine gun still chattered on, quivering under my fingers, throwing out six hundred slugs a minute. The belt ran its course and silence fell like a curtain across the smoke-blued interior.

Men were sprawled in queerly twisted heaps before me. Something shiny was running through the cracks in the stones. The smoking torch sputtered on.

Sheila was there beside me, trying to lift me away from the wall. "El Zidan is coming!" she cried urgently. "McKenna deserted to the other fort to give them the orders!"

The knowledge that I had to do something about it was like a cold shower. I remember staring stupidly at the waiting stallion, trying to summon nerve enough to get up. I suppose I was afraid to move, afraid of what I might find out.

Sheila was dragging a box toward me, her gold hair cascading about her, getting across her vision. She was tangled up in smoke and the dull lethargy which persisted in settling in upon me.

"Quick, Eddie! We've got to do something! They'll slaughter them!"

Somehow I climbed to my feet and steadied myself by

holding the stallion's bridle. The constant warmth along my side was terrifying. My right boot was squashy as I stepped.

I saw the contents of the box then. It held musettes full of hand grenades. I managed to throw a bag over my arm. By gritting my teeth I climbed up on the Arabian.

He took the steps, cautiously setting out one foot at a time. The musette banged against my thigh. I could hear the drumming of hoofs and the cries of men. A shot rang out as sharp as breaking glass.

El Zidan and Nicolle were less than a thousand yards away—and coming fast!

I watched the opposite fort and saw no sign of life. They were waiting silently to spring the trap. Machine guns at close range are deadly in effect.

The stallion trotted toward the gates of the Black City. I remember staring at the moon, wondering if I'd live long enough to see it get all the way over the horizon. There was something terribly vital about seeing that moon.

When I was below the other fort, I saw I had accomplished my purpose. Those in the kasbah were unwilling to give away their position just for the sake of shooting one man. And they thought I had no direct interest in them.

I wheeled the stallion. He snorted as I jabbed the spurs. He plunged toward the fort, a white javelin in the blue gloom.

The walls began to rear up before me. I held my breath, wondering when they would begin to fire. They must think me mad. They would hardly expect me to do any real damage to them.

A rifle spat from an embrasure. I reined to one side. Another cracked. El Zidan was within five hundred yards and coming like a white avalanche. A machine gun began to clatter on the kasbah roof. I saw one of El Zidan's troopers go down in a skidding swirl of dust.

And then I was tight in under the wall of the fort, below their angle of depression. They couldn't hit me here unless they leaned all the way out of the embrasure.

Pulling the grenade pins with my teeth, I threw them up in a soaring arc. They went as rapidly as I could jerk them out of the bag. Sometimes I could see them silhouetted against the sky when they hung at the top of their trajectory.

The entire pass lighted up. The embrasure caved. Stones showered about me. The exploding grenades began their deafening cannonade. Sections of guns and walls and men soared upward.

I heard a small, piping cry through the maelstrom of sound: "*Illahu!* Allah the All Merciful—"

I was swept up by a thunder of hoofs and a sea of djellabas. I caught a swift impression of khaki-clad men running toward the gates.

El Zidan, a towering, roaring man on a plunging horse caught me before I fell out of my saddle. Numb and sticky and tired, I let him throw me across his pommel. Above me I saw the gates loom, heard the hammering of rifle butts against wood.

And then the shattered gates were under us and we were pouring into the Black City. Men stood up before us and went down before the onslaught of autorifles, Sniders and grenades. The barking Lebels ripped into the jammed pass mouth. Legion Hotchkiss guns yammered from the remaining fort.

I faintly remember El Zidan as he let me down to a step. His djellaba swirled and he was gone.

By turning my head a little I could see the round disc of the moon swimming up, blotting out the stars with light. Sheila Gordon's head was silhouetted by the glow.

CHAPTER TEN

A Letter to the Vice-Consul

NICOLLE, slapping his boots with his riding crop, paced up and down the room. Occasionally he raked me with his glare. I was propped up on a stack of pillows, slightly drunk from an overdose of Hasan's morphine, given very much against my protests.

With a Legionnaire on either side of him, Abu 'l Hasan sat in a chair against the wall.

El Zidan leaned lazily against the window ledge and watched the smoke roll out of his cigarette. From the polish of his red boots and spurs and from the white silkiness of his djellaba, it was hard to believe that he had fought like a madman the night before.

Sheila Gordon had seated herself in the corner, out of the way. Her blue eyes were bright and watchful.

"Nicolle," said El Zidan, "you have the facts, and you know that I wouldn't lie to France."

"No question about lying," crackled Nicolle, tweaking his spiked mustache. "I am merely surprised beyond all reason at the outcome of this matter."

"No use to be surprised," I said. "The facts are all before you."

"Perhaps they are," said Nicolle, "but I don't like the looks of the facts. And besides, how can I guarantee the peace of this— How can I guarantee *your* attitude toward France?"

"I love France," said El Zidan, smiling and shifting his boots so that the spurs tinkled. "I love France with all my heart and soul."

Nicolle turned on Abu 'l Hasan.

"And what have *you* to say for yourself?"

"I swear," bellowed Hasan, "that this is all a mistake. I did not know I was attacking the French Foreign Legion."

"No," said Nicolle with honey-covered sarcasm, "your eyes did not tell you that you fired upon and ultimately charged men dressed in khaki who bore the red and blue! Oh, never mind the explanation, Hasan. This matter— It puzzles me still, why you should think yourself great enough to fight French troops when you have pledged such great allegiance to France."

Hasan's vulture eyes were deadly as he glared at me.

"This Moran," he said, "told me that El Zidan had dressed his men as Legionnaires and that El Zidan was about to attack the Black City."

I began to laugh, and when Nicolle looked at me, he too smiled.

"A very likely tale, Hasan," said Nicolle. "I think it best that I take you to Fez to let a French tribunal try your crime. Why, if it had not been for El Zidan's help in that emergency, I would have been wiped out!"

El Zidan smiled modestly.

"Remember, *Capitaine,* that I merely kept you from killing me off. I did not slay any of your troops."

"That's very true," replied Nicolle. "And I appreciate your

tact in the matter. Legionnaires! Take this Hasan down to the anteroom and wait for me."

When Hasan had gone, protesting and at last wailing, Nicolle turned to El Zidan.

"You say his troops have pledged loyalty to you. I think then that I can trust you to keep peace in this region and to govern your kingdom well. I have no authority to turn this over to you, but as you are the real ruler, I see no harm. And as for you, Moran, I will have a *cacolet* made up."

"A mule stretcher!" I cried. "I'm bled white now!"

"But I must take you back for trans-shipment to French Indochina."

El Zidan flipped the ashes from his cigarette.

"Have a care, *Capitaine*. You are talking to my grand vizier."

"What's this?" gasped Nicolle.

"My grand vizier will hereafter be addressed as His Excellency. The audience is over, Nicolle. I will send suitable cavalry to escort you back through the pass."

El Zidan's broad shoulders bulged beneath the djellaba. His face and eyes were very stern. Nicolle snapped his heels together and saluted. El Zidan bowed easily.

Nicolle paused on his way to the door.

"A pleasant rule, El Zidan," he said, "and a rapid recovery, Your Excellency."

I nodded solemnly and when Nicolle had gone, I turned to Sheila. "Sheila, there's some paper and ink over on that desk. Will you write a letter for me?"

"Certainly, Your Excellency!" She laughed as she sat down.

"To," I said, "Godfrey Harrison. 'Dear Sir: Some years ago, I believe I heard you say you wanted to have a legation or an embassy. I am now offering you the post of ambassador to the Black Kingdom—'"

"Wait," interrupted El Zidan. "I don't like Black Kingdom. I'm going to have everything painted white."

I continued— "'the White Kingdom. Have this matter arranged immediately and come down here for a visit while we iron out the diplomacies of the matter. Also, my dear Godfrey, there are nothing but Mohammedan Marabouts here and I find myself very much in need of the services of a Christian minister. Rush one along with you, or send him parcel post. I sincerely hope—'"

McKenna, very much bandaged, thrust his shaggy eyebrows through the door. "Begging your pardon, sirs, but I was wondering—"

"Go back and give a barrel of oats to the white stallion," I said. "And give him a good rubdown. And hereafter don't come busting around when you aren't called."

"Yes, sir!"

"Now, Sheila," I said, "you can end that letter with: 'And I sincerely hope to be seeing you soon, especially with that minister. Yours very truly, His Excellency, Eddie Moran, General of Armies, Admiral of Navies, Grand Vizier of the White Kingdom.'"

Escape for Three

Escape for Three

"T HEY'VE got him, the swine," growled Blucher, the Hun.

"Serves the ugly cockroach right," said Santos, the Saint.

"He's paying now for all the hell he's dished out himself," agreed John Smith, the Yank.

All three sat and nodded to each other in silent satisfaction. No other occurrence less than finding a million dollars could have pleased them so much as the capture of Lieutenant Moraine by the hill Berbers. In their eyes were mirrored their gloating thoughts. Lieutenant Moraine was being given a dose of his own pills.

He was an arrogant fool, that Moraine. Haughty and rich, fresh from the Spahis. He didn't and never would belong in the Legion. He didn't understand a Legionnaire. He'd been known to sentence men to polishing his boots and that was unforgivable even to a *bleu*. He'd picked up ideas of field punishment in England and torture fitted it better. He thought he was a little metal god set up to be worshiped by the soldiers who served France but were not French.

And Moraine hated the Legion and that was worse. He thought he was too good for such service. He considered all Legionnaires to be some particularly filthy species of pig, and what was worse, said so.

And then he was too handsome for a man. He was beautiful.

The thoughts of the three, sitting there on the parapet of the hastily built fort, surrounded by the glamour and silence of the Moroccan night, did not match the beauty of the stars.

"They'll gouge out his pretty eyes," said Blucher, the Hun.

"And stick twigs through his smoothly shaven cheeks," added Santos, the Saint.

"Yeah," said John Smith in a gleeful voice, "And they'll turn him over to their women for the finishing touches."

Moraine had been taken in a skirmish that afternoon. He had been trapped alone and had been led away to the Berber strongholds higher in the hills. It might be all over by this time.

"But it's too bad," said Blucher, shaking his thick head. "He had so much money and influence. We could have used that. LeBrun isn't much better than Moraine and I'm sick of this."

"I'm sick, too," said Santos. He looked narrowly at his two friends. He had the face of a devil when he looked like that. He was dark and evil and he liked the night best.

"Yeah," said John Smith, leaning forward. "Say, do you suppose—"

"No," said Blucher. "They've killed him by now."

"But," said Smith, "if they haven't, then . . . Think of the money he's got, huh? Now, if the three of us could get hold of him and—"

"Force him to take us to Casablanca and buy our way—"

"That's right," said Blucher. "If we got hold of him, we could make him do anything."

"I wonder," said Santos.

They moved nervously, certain that LeBrun would be there listening.

"He's a fool," said Smith. "He stood up there like a signpost and told us to come on. He knew he'd be cut off. That's a showoff for you."

"He knew he looked pretty that way," said Santos.

"Think we could take him?" ventured Blucher.

"Sure we could. Listen, the Berbers don't know all the tortures and they wouldn't be expecting three guys to sneak up and cop a prisoner." Smith leaned heavily forward again. "We get him out, make him lead the way to Casablanca, demand ten thousand dollars apiece for his life—"

"And then kill him," decided Santos.

"Okay," said Smith.

"I'm sick of this," agreed Blucher.

"Done," said Santos.

With an elaborate show of weariness, they stood up and stretched, and wandered toward their small tents which perched precariously upon the hillside. Everyone but the sentries slept the sleep of tired fighting men. They met beside the parapet a few minutes later with full water bottles and food-crammed knapsacks. They carried their Lebels in both hands as men do when they expect trouble.

"Lead off," said Smith.

"No," said Blucher in a whisper which shook a little. "You go first."

"Okay," said Smith and eased over the low wall.

A rock rolled underfoot and a sentry's sling snapped briskly.

"Qu'est-ce que c'est?"

"Goin' for a drink," replied Smith, hidden by blue darkness.

The sentry's gun butt thumped back to the ground and they heard him sigh with boredom.

The hillside was steep and at times they had to crawl backwards on all fours, carefully placing their guns flat down on the hard, dry earth each time. They had no wish to announce their presence by jingling equipment.

The Berbers were not far away. Berber sentries, they knew, would be stationed through the darkness to prevent just such a thing happening. But Berbers expected Legionnaires to be regular and punctual, attacking as before at dawn.

It was chilly. A cold wind was coming down from the snows of Mount Tirzah. The desert was thousands of feet below and hundreds of kilometers away. The Legionnaires had pushed deep this time. Berber resistance to French colonization would be put down once and forever. The khaki lines of stubborn fighting men had already bowed Berber resistance, bent it almost to breaking.

Smith led down a gully and climbed up toward a knife ridge which loomed against the incredible stars.

"They took him this way," said Santos. "But how will we find the right place? There are thousands of Berbers—"

"We'll get a man and make him talk," promised Blucher.

"I wonder why we never thought of this before," said Smith. "It's so easy."

"Sure it's easy," agreed Santos. "Until we run into Berbers. They can shoot like the devil at night. I saw—"

"Shut up," said Blucher.

Smith mounted the ridge and looked down on the other side. Then he signaled and dropped over. They were nearing the scene of their most recent engagement.

Something white moved stealthily before them. They stopped, their ragged khaki and dust-grimed faces blending perfectly with the hillside.

"Raiding party," whispered Smith.

The Berbers were three in number, out to see how many French throats they could cut before dawn, out to roll a few grenades under the tent flaps of the sleeping *Franzawi*—if they could.

"Take 'em in order," whispered Smith.

The hazy blur of the three djellabas came slowly forward. The Berbers did not expect trouble almost in their own lines. They came on, pushing their mountain guns ahead of them, making their way up the steep hill like goats.

Smith moved a little closer to the spot the first would pass. He waited there. Two men went by him so close he could smell rancid butter and decayed goat flesh. The third was big, looking like an animated circus tent.

Smith held his breath and then, in a voice like a whip-crack, he said, "Now!"

Smith lunged forward, hand already reaching out to still the yell which started up from the Berber's chest. Smith's bayonet flashed and then didn't flash. It rasped as he drew it across his man's throat.

Blucher was shaking his man, holding him clear of the ground. Santos was underneath and the Berber was fighting too hard to cry out. Smith sank his bayonet between the Berber's shoulder blades and pulled Santos out from under.

Santos and Smith seized Blucher's man and threw him down. The fellow's eyes were white spots in the blackness of night. His white skin was too dirty to glow.

Santos went to work. He took a strip from a djellaba and bound it loosely about the Berber's head. Santos thrust his scabbard through the loop and began to turn it like a tourniquet. The band grew tighter and tighter above the Berber's eyes. But he could not squall his pain. Smith's hand prevented that.

The cloth stretched and creaked. The Berber's eyes were starting from his head as though driven from within. The band would soon split his head open. Already he suffered unbearable pain.

Santos talked Shilha to him. "Where is the *Franzawi* officer? Quick, answer or we spill out your brains."

The Berber moaned. Santos tightened the band.

"Take your hand away," whispered Santos. "He can't talk with your hand there, you idiot."

Smith removed his hand.

"Where is the officer?" said Santos.

"In the camp. In the camp. He is in the hut of a captain of one hundred."

"You know the hut?"

"Yes, yes, I know it. Allah, Allah, you will crack my head open. You will murder me!"

"Lead away," said Santos, keeping the scabbard tightly in place.

Santos talked Shilha to him. "Where is the Franzawi officer? Quick, answer or we spill out your brains."

Evidently the man's eyes were too hazed with pain to let him see. He stumbled and tripped and wandered off to the side of the path he had chosen. Santos loosened the cloth a little and they made better progress.

Before long they were challenged in Shilha by a white ghost.

"We come with news," answered Santos.

The Berber stepped closer, suspiciously. Blucher laid open his head with a rifle butt and kicked the body off the trail. They went on.

Ahead they could see the walls of a settlement looming up. The mountain town was quiet save for a dog that whined incessantly and a horse that stamped.

At the gates, Santos stopped and whispered, "We're through their lines."

"Of course, you fool," said Blucher. "Go in."

"You go in," said Santos.

Smith shouldered past and looked about for a sentry. But the Berbers evidently had faith in their numbers who guarded the slopes. Smith felt disappointed. He had expected a sharp fight. It had been too easy.

The Berber, with the cloth tightened again, pointed out the house they wanted. They shoved him forward. The dog still whined.

The hut was dark, the doors were open. Confidently, Smith stepped across the threshold—and squarely in the middle of a Berber's belly.

The man yelled and leaped up. Smith jabbed with the heel of his gun and turned the face into a bloody mass. The man they had captured took the opportunity to twist free and run, shrieking.

Instantly the camp was up and moving. But the escaping Berber did not get far. Santos lunged with his bayonet and yanked the fellow back into the hut.

Santos worked fast. He slipped the dead man's tunic off and flung it over his head. Then he ran out, shooting and swearing in Shilha.

"They'll get away!" screamed Santos.

Moving hoods and capes quickly launched themselves toward him, following him, shouting.

"The *Franzawi!*" cried Santos.

Smith stared through a slit in the door. "They're running after him," breathed Smith.

"The fool," snapped Blucher. "They'll know he isn't a Berber."

But Santos ran on, shooting his rifle and yelling. In a moment, every man in the village was streaming along in his wake. The dog had given over whining now. He was howling. The horses jerked their heads excitedly and tried to shed their halters.

Smith turned back to the two dead Berbers. A third man cowered in the corner of the hut. Blucher jerked him forward and clipped him on the jaw with an iron fist. The Berber sagged, unconscious, to the floor.

"They'll have killed him by now," sighed Blucher.

Smith looked into a second room and found what they sought.

Lieutenant Moraine was lying inertly upon the bare floor,

facing the wall, bound hand and foot. A patch of starlight caught in his insignia and sparkled. His khaki was torn, and blood stained the side of his handsome head.

Blucher pulled Moraine into a sitting position and, with a bayonet, quickly cut away the grass ropes. Moraine looked empty and sick. His black eyes were without luster and he looked at the two Legionnaires without seeing them at all. A bullet had plowed along his jaw, forever destroying the beauty of his face. He was a welter of dried blood and bruises—but the Berbers had not tortured him.

Rudely, Smith slapped Moraine upon the arm and shook him hard. "Come awake. Snap into it, *mon lieutenant*. It's Blucher and Smith."

Moraine gazed at them for precious seconds and then something of understanding came over his face, but he was still dazed.

"What do you want?"

Blucher sent a grin toward Smith. "You'll find out later. Get up!"

Moraine managed to stand but his well-shaped body drooped. Smith shoved a dirty gray djellaba at him and then, when the lieutenant merely looked at it, made haste to put it on the man.

Blucher dressed in the second cloak. There was none for Smith.

They went out into the other room. The door creaked and their hands sought their rifles. The hooded head which entered spoke French. It was Santos.

"They're way down the trail, still running," chuckled Santos.

"Quickly, I've got the horses."

They went out again into the starlight. The village was deserted except for the howling dog. Santos had brought four Moorish barbs up before the hut. The mounts stood wild-eyed and shying, unused to the smell of Frenchmen.

Moraine was staggering, lightheaded from pain and loss of blood. But when he mounted he managed a smile at them. Blucher winked at Santos when he saw it.

"Now for Casablanca," whispered Smith excitedly.

"Casablanca," echoed Santos.

They seized the bridle of Moraine's mount and led off at a trot. Smith, uneasy in his khaki, brought up the rear.

It appeared for a few minutes that they would make it without any trouble, and then the Berbers ahead, who had been led astray by Santos, realized that they had been duped and turned back in anger upon hearing from the sentries that no *Franzawi* had passed.

The black gorge before them suddenly turned white with gray figures. With a startled shout, two Berbers were jostled off the trail by the lead horse.

Santos yelled something appropriately insulting but in his excitement, he said it in *French*!

Instantly mountain rifles exploded. Moraine's horse went down squealing in agony. Smith scooped up the lieutenant before the officer touched dirt.

With kicking heels and slapping hands the Legionnaires urged their barbs into the milling throng before them. Santos and Blucher struck to the right and left with clubbed rifles. Men pressed in against them to be trodden under by rearing hoofs.

Steel clanged against bayonet. Powder flame lit up the pass like lightning. Santos cried out and clutched drunkenly at the crosstree of his Berber saddle.

Smith, hampered by the lieutenant, fired with his rifle held against his side. Men went down shot after shot. The trail was soft with bodies. Hands tore at the Legionnaires, striving to pull them under.

Santos dragged himself upright and fumbled in his djellaba hood. The man he had taken it from had carried grenades for use against the *Franzawi*. Santos pulled the pin and did not wait to count. In spite of the agony the throw cost him, he pitched the corrugated ellipsoid far ahead of them.

The flash and thunder was like a physical blow. Fragments of steel sang over their heads. Berbers were blown into atoms. Santos threw again and again. It sounded like a rolling barrage.

Suddenly the Berbers fell away with cries of fear. They did not quite understand. It was too dark. They had a half-formed idea that they were being assailed from the rear.

With shouts the three Legionnaires galloped ahead, down the trail toward their own camp. The sound of their passage was drowned in the cries which went up all along the slope of the mountain. But once out of the press, they were lost to the Berbers. The three rode too fast and too determinedly.

They paid no attention to one another. As one man they headed for the French lines. And after fifteen minutes of hard riding they flung themselves off their horses and toiled up the slope toward the parapet they had so lately quit.

Smith had Moraine over his shoulder and Moraine was protesting that he could walk. Smith paid no attention to that.

The camp had already heard the firing and the parapet was lined with anxious, tired faces behind ready guns. But when the men saw the uniform of Smith the guns went down and a shout went up.

Eager hands dragged the quartet over the wall and many voices hammered questions and cried acclaim.

It was some hours before dawn, but it took the three Legionnaires all that time to satisfy the curiosity of the camp by telling the story over and over again.

The next morning Smith wandered over to the medical tent to see how Moraine was doing. The officer grinned at him from a cocoon of bandages and then remembered that he was an officer.

"Good work, Smith," said Moraine.

"Thanks," said Smith. That was all. He went out again and found Blucher and Santos. The two were grinning at him.

"It's a bad soldier that doesn't growl," said Blucher.

"Yeah," said Santos, mimicking Smith.

Smith looked long at them and then broke into a loud laugh. "I thought—I thought that you guys—"

"I know," said Santos. "You thought that Blucher and I wanted to desert and decided to use us in rescuing Moraine. We thought the same thing about you."

"But the point is," said Blucher, "whatever we thought, Moraine is here again."

They laughed together for several seconds and then, growing somewhat embarrassed as men do when accused of heroism, they changed the subject and sat down upon the parapet.

"He's a swine," said Smith. "All he could say was 'Thanks.'"

"He told me my coat was unbuttoned," growled Blucher.

"If they'd killed him," said Santos, "it would have served him right."

Story Preview

NOW that you've just ventured through some of the captivating tales in the Stories from the Golden Age collection by L. Ron Hubbard, turn the page and enjoy a preview of *Trick Soldier*. Join two Marines in the midst of a fierce rebel uprising in the Haitian jungle, pitted against each other with a bitter and deadly score to settle.

Trick Soldier

T HEY stood looking at each other through the hot haze of evening, and as they stared ten years went by and they saw again the swirling dust of parade grounds and heard the monotonous voice of a drill sergeant counting cadence.

Ten years and three thousand miles to that sweaty field, but they bridged it and the jungle about them faded away, their bars were forgotten, their formalities swept aside by recognition. They were once again "boots," not *gendarmerie* captain and *gendarmerie* lieutenant.

Brittle gray eyes clashed with arrogant brown ones. Fists doubled into white-knuckled knots.

The new arrival had said, saluting briskly, "Lieutenant Flint reports to Captain Turner for . . ." And then he had seen. His hand had dropped insolently, his mouth had curled thickly and recognition had come.

Captain Turner's own hand had stopped halfway to his helmet. He too had remembered. And there they stood, facing each other, rank, jungle, command all thrown aside.

"They . . . they sent me you," muttered Turner. "You!"

Flint's dark face relaxed into a malicious smile. His glance roved up and down the *gendarmerie* captain, slowly, hatefully. "Turner," said Flint, his voice thick. "Turner the trick soldier.

So you're here, huh? So they boosted you up, huh? *Captain* Turner, is it?"

Flint studied the smaller man. Turner's face was finely molded, the face of a gentleman. Turner wore a small, spiked mustache, waxed to perfection. Turner's shirt was obviously tailored, fitting in close to his slim hips. The man wore lace boots instead of leggings, and the boots were cordovan mirrors. Even the khaki tie looked stiff, too perfect.

"*Captain* Turner," repeated Flint with a hard, ugly laugh. "The trick soldier. Boots, starch and wax." Thereupon, Flint unfastened his tie and opened his collar, letting his beet-red throat shine through the gap. He removed his pith helmet with its black inverted chevron—the insignia of second lieutenant in the *Gendarmerie d'Haiti*—and thrust it under his arm. He took out a greasy handkerchief and swabbed at his narrow brow.

"And I marched all this way in all this rig, just to report to *you!*" Flint let his mouth curl with disdain as though he smelled something very odorous.

Turner straightened his spine. His nostrils quivered. "Attention, you fool! Take a hitch in that collar and put on your hat. I don't care if you're Jesus Christ, I'm in command here and you're to be second in command. *Second,* do you hear me? Attention, I said. Those devils are watching us. Do you want to wreck half a year's work in this damned jungle? Now, salute and report."

Flint looked down upon the smaller man. Flint's shoulders bulged under his issue shirt, Flint's neck swelled as his anger mounted.

Flint's close-set eyes, sunken into his bloated face, drew tight until only the dark pupil showed. "Military martinet. Trick soldier. Aw, get the hell off your high horse. This is the jungle. We're fifteen miles from Cap-Haïtien. We're lost as far as the regiment is concerned."

Insolently he looked at the men who stood in a semicircle, at a respectful distance behind their commander. These men were soldiers of the *gendarmerie*, native Haitians, trained and temporarily commanded by transferred officers of the Marine Corps. Because they considered all whites as lower in the social scale, because they would even refuse to defile themselves by eating with a white man, they were hard to command, hard to keep under discipline.

But Flint grinned at them and caught the returning flash of white teeth in ebon faces. "Native soldiers," commented Flint, "commanded by a tin general." He gave a sudden start.

Turner's black .45 had been swinging on his hip, flap buckled back, allowing the butt to protrude. The automatic was now in Turner's slender, small-boned hand and the muzzle was trained on Flint's brass belt buckle which glinted in the patterns of sunlight that filtered through the trees.

"Salute," said Turner. "Fast!"

Flint goggled at the gun and then replaced his hat. When he started to raise his hand, Turner rapped, "Fasten your tie. Button up those pockets."

Flint buttoned the pockets and arranged the tie. Then, his size-eighteen neck straining at the collar, mouth warped in a half smile, he said in a mocking voice, "Lieutenant Flint wishes to report to Captain Turner, commanding Company X, *gendarmerie*. Lieutenant Flint requests an assignment to quarters and duties."

"Go into my tent," said Turner, putting the gun away. "I must clear out MacLeod's quarters for the lieutenant's occupancy."

Flint looked at the men and grinned again. Then he bowed his head and entered the small field tent which faced the cleared square, the drill ground of the post.

Turner's palms were sweaty, but not from heat. He was nervous. He turned on the men. "Get to your quarters!" he barked, and they scattered.

Walking with stiff, uncompromising stride, the diminutive Turner made his way to a tent some thirty feet away from his own. Behind the tent, watched over by a rudely lashed cross, was a red rectangle, bare earth, startling and gruesome against the green.

Turner entered the tent, trying not to glance at the blazoned earth. Not twenty-four hours past he had buried Sergeant MacLeod there. Lieutenant MacLeod of the *gendarmerie*.

The field locker was open beside the cot. The white blankets with USN stamped upon them were spread neatly on the bed, ready to be unrolled. A Springfield, shiny with polishing and burnishing, hung from the edge of the cot, upside down. A belted holster, sagging under the weight of the .45, coiled over the edge of an ammunition case MacLeod had used for a desk and dressing table. The razor, wiped dry, was laid out, ready for use. A cake of red soap was still damp in its saucer.

Turner stopped in the dim interior and stared about him.

His chest was leaden. A girl's face stared at him from the opened locker, smiling with promise—for MacLeod.

Turner's knees felt wobbly. He seated himself on the cot and stared at the girl for a space of minutes. Then he fumbled with the Springfield's lashing and saw that his hands shook. He sat still again, looking back at the girl.

Twenty-four hours before, MacLeod had died with the sun, his chest ripped open by a soft-nosed slug, never regaining consciousness. He had been killed on patrol, from ambush, by the *cacos*. He had been buried at sundown without taps, with a few half-remembered phrases, wrapped in an OD blanket, six feet down in the sticky clay soil.

Turner started. He thought he heard MacLeod's explosive laugh outside. He had been hearing it for six months, and now he would hear it no more. But the echos were still there, haunting him.

To find out more about *Trick Soldier* and how you can obtain your copy, go to www.goldenagestories.com.

Glossary

STORIES FROM THE GOLDEN AGE *reflect the words and expressions used in the 1930s and 1940s, adding unique flavor and authenticity to the tales. While a character's speech may often reflect regional origins, it also can convey attitudes common in the day. So that readers can better grasp such cultural and historical terms, uncommon words or expressions of the era, the following glossary has been provided.*

Annamite: of Annam, a French protectorate encompassing the central region of Vietnam. The region was seized by the French and became part of French Indochina in 1887. It regained its independence in 1945.

AVB rifle grenade: anti-personnel VB (for Viven-Bessières, the French company that made it) rifle grenade; a form of grenade that utilizes a rifle as a launch mechanism to increase the effective range of the grenade.

barbs: a breed of horses introduced by the Moors (Muslim people of mixed Berber and Arab descent) that resemble Arabian horses and are known for their speed and endurance.

Berber: a member of a people living in North Africa, primarily Muslim, living in settled or nomadic tribes between the

Sahara and Mediterranean Sea and between Egypt and the Atlantic Ocean.

bleu: (French) a new recruit; newcomer.

boots: Marine or Navy recruits in basic training.

Browning: a .30- or .50-caliber automatic belt-fed, air-cooled or water-cooled machine gun capable of firing ammunition at a rate of more than 500 rounds per minute.

burg: city or town.

cacolet: (French) a horse or mule litter for the transport of wounded.

cacos: (French) loosely knit bandit organizations who hired out to the highest bidder. The transfer of power in Haiti traditionally occurred when a political contender raised a *caco* army and marched on the capital. The transfer was completed when the incumbent fled the country with part of the treasury.

cantle: the raised back part of a saddle for a horse.

Cap-Haïtien: a main city on the north coast of Haiti facing the Atlantic Ocean.

carbine: a short light rifle; originally used by soldiers on horseback.

Casablanca: a seaport on the Atlantic coast of Morocco.

concha: a disk, traditionally of hammered silver and resembling a shell or flower, used as a decoration piece on belts, harnesses, etc.

cop: to steal something, especially by snatching it hurriedly.

corrugated ellipsoid: an oval shape with parallel and alternating ridges and grooves; grenade.

coup de soleil: (French) sunburn.

crosstree: the raised wooden pieces at the front and rear of the saddle that form a high pommel or horn in the front and cantle in the back.

djellaba: a long loose hooded garment with full sleeves, worn especially in Muslim countries.

dum-dum: a bullet with a soft front that increases in size when it hits its target, causing serious injuries.

Fez: the former capital of several dynasties and one of the holiest places in Morocco; it has kept its religious primacy through the ages.

flintlock: a type of gun fired by a spark from a flint (rock used with steel to produce an igniting spark). It was introduced about 1630.

forty-five or **.45:** a handgun chambered to fire a .45-caliber cartridge and that utilizes the recoil or part of the force of the explosive to eject the spent cartridge shell, introduce a new cartridge, cock the arm and fire it repeatedly.

.45 Colt: a .45-caliber automatic pistol manufactured by the Colt Firearms Company of Hartford, Connecticut. Colt was founded by Samuel Colt (1814–1862), who revolutionized the firearms industry.

Franzawi: (Arabic) Frenchman.

French Foreign Legion: a unique elite unit within the French Army established in 1831. It was created as a unit for foreign volunteers and was primarily used to protect and expand the French colonial empire during the nineteenth century, but has also taken part in all of France's wars with other European powers. It is known to be an elite military unit whose training focuses not only on traditional military skills, but also on the building of a strong esprit de corps amongst members. As its men come from different countries with different cultures, this is a widely accepted solution to strengthen them enough to work as a team. Training is often not only physically hard with brutal training methods, but also extremely stressful with high rates of desertion.

French Indochina: part of the French colonial empire in Indochina, a region in southeast Asia, east of India and south of China.

Frogs: Frenchmen.

Gendarmerie d'Haiti: (French) police force of Haiti. Organized in 1916, and initially consisting of 250 officers and 2,500 men, their purpose was to provide police services throughout the country. The *gendarmerie* was officered by Marine Corps personnel, most of whom were sergeants with officer rank in the Haitian service. The *gendarmerie* fought alongside Marine occupying forces during the *caco* wars.

G-men: government men; agents of the Federal Bureau of Investigation.

Haitian: of Haiti, country in the Caribbean occupying the western part of the island of Hispaniola. The other half is occupied by the Dominican Republic.

Hamitic: of or relating to the Hamites, African people of Caucasoid descent believed to be the original settlers of northern Africa from Asia.

heliograph: a device for signaling by means of a movable mirror that reflects beams of light, especially sunlight, to a distance.

High Atlas: portion of the Atlas Mountain range that rises in the west at the Atlantic coast and stretches in an eastern direction to the Moroccan-Algerian border.

Hotchkiss: a heavy machine gun designed and manufactured by the Hotchkiss Company in France from the late 1920s until World War II. The machine gun is named for Benjamin B. Hotchkiss (1826–1885), one of the leading American weapons engineers of his day who established the company in 1867.

ifrīt: (Arabic) a powerful evil *jinnī,* demon or monstrous giant in Arabic mythology.

illahu: (Arabic) *al illahu;* the (one) God.

Imaziren: an indigenous people of Morocco who are Berbers and who call themselves Imaziren (free-men).

jinnī or *jinn:* (Arabic) *jinnī* singular, *jinn* plural; in Muslim legend, a spirit often capable of assuming human or animal form and exercising supernatural influence over people.

kasbah: a castle built on a high place to defend a North African city.

la belle Légion: (French) the lovely Legion.

Lebel: a French rifle that was adopted as a standard infantry weapon in 1887 and remained in official service until after World War II.

legation: the official headquarters of a diplomatic minister.

Legion: French Foreign Legion.

Legionnaire: a member of the French Foreign Legion.

limned: outlined in clear detail; delineated.

Magat: a river on the largest island of the Philippines.

Mannlicher: a type of rifle equipped with a manually operated sliding bolt for loading cartridges as opposed to the more common rotating bolt of other rifles. Mannlicher rifles were considered reasonably strong and accurate.

Marabouts: spiritual leaders in the Islamic faith, especially in Africa. They are scholars of the Koran and many make amulets for good luck, preside at various ceremonies and in some cases actively guide the life of the follower.

martinet: a rigid military disciplinarian.

mon ami: (French) my friend.

mon lieutenant: (French) my lieutenant.

Monsieur: (French) Mr.

Moorish: of the Moors, Muslim people of mixed Berber and Arab descent.

Moroccan: of Morocco, a country in North Africa. It has a coast on the Atlantic Ocean that reaches past the Strait of Gibraltar into the Mediterranean Sea.

mountain rifle: a very long, ruggedly built rifle designed for use in mountainous terrain.

musette: a small canvas or leather bag with a shoulder strap, as one used by soldiers or travelers.

OD: (military) olive drab.

offal: refuse; rubbish.

parapet: a wall, rampart or elevation of earth for covering soldiers from an enemy's fire.

pith helmet: a lightweight hat made from dried pith, the soft spongelike tissue in the stems of most flowering plants.

Pith helmets are worn in tropical countries for protection from the sun.

present arms: a position in which a long gun, such as a rifle, is held perpendicularly in front of the center of the body.

Qu'est-ce que c'est?: (French) What is that?

rowels: the small spiked revolving wheels on the ends of spurs, which are attached to the heels of a rider's boots and used to nudge a horse into going faster.

run-over: of boots, where the heel is so unevenly worn on the outside that the back of the boot starts to lean to one side and does not sit straight above the heel.

salāt: (Arabic) a ritual Muslim prayer made five times a day (dawn, midday, afternoon, evening and night) in a standing position, alternating with inclinations and prostrations, as the worshiper faces toward Mecca.

Scheherazade: the female narrator of *The Arabian Nights,* who during one thousand and one adventurous nights saved her life by entertaining her husband, the king, with stories.

scimitar: a curved, single-edged sword of Oriental origin.

Shaitan: (Arabic) Satan.

Shilha: the Berber dialect spoken in the mountains of southern Morocco.

Snider: a rifle formerly used in the British service. It was invented by American Jacob Snider in the mid-1800s. The Snider was a breech-loading rifle, derived from its muzzle-loading predecessor called the Enfield.

sorrel: a horse with a reddish-brown coat.

Spahis: light cavalry regiments of the French Army recruited primarily from Algeria, Tunisia and Morocco.

Springfield: any of several types of rifle, named after Springfield, Massachusetts, the site of a federal armory that made the rifles.

tramp: a freight vessel that does not run regularly between fixed ports, but takes a cargo wherever shippers desire.

trick soldier: a soldier who, in the convention of military dress and duties, is conspicuously smart, attractive, effective or able.

vizier: a high officer in a Muslim government.

Wagon-Lit: name of a hotel. Wagon-Lit means "sleeping car" in French. Sleeping compartments on trains were first introduced by Georges Nagelmackers in 1872 to service international railroad travelers on trains such as the Orient Express. The original company, Campaignie Internationale des Wagons-Lits, later expanded into hotels.

Webley: Webley and Scott handgun; an arms manufacturer based in England that produced handguns from 1834. Webley is famous for the revolvers and automatic pistols it supplied to the British Empire's military from 1887 through World War I and World War II.

wudu': (Arabic) a Muslim cleansing ritual involving cleaning with water of the hands, face, mouth and feet (and perhaps other parts of the body), which is a symbol of spiritual cleansing. Usually practiced before *salāt.*

Yank: Yankee; term used to refer to Americans in general.

Zouave: a member of a French infantry unit, originally composed of Algerian recruits and characterized by colorful uniforms with baggy trousers.

L. Ron Hubbard
in the Golden Age
of Pulp Fiction

*In writing an adventure story
a writer has to know that he is adventuring
for a lot of people who cannot.
The writer has to take them here and there
about the globe and show them
excitement and love and realism.
As long as that writer is living the part of an
adventurer when he is hammering
the keys, he is succeeding with his story.*

*Adventuring is a state of mind.
If you adventure through life, you have a
good chance to be a success on paper.*

*Adventure doesn't mean globe-trotting,
exactly, and it doesn't mean great deeds.
Adventuring is like art.
You have to live it to make it real.*

— *L. RON HUBBARD*

L. Ron Hubbard
and American
Pulp Fiction

B ORN March 13, 1911, L. Ron Hubbard lived a life at
least as expansive as the stories with which he enthralled
a hundred million readers through a fifty-year career.

Originally hailing from Tilden, Nebraska, he spent his
formative years in a classically rugged Montana, replete with
the cowpunchers, lawmen and desperadoes who would later
people his Wild West adventures. And lest anyone imagine
those adventures were drawn from vicarious experience, he
was not only breaking broncs at a tender age, he was also
among the few whites ever admitted into Blackfoot society
as a bona fide blood brother. While if only to round out an
otherwise rough and tumble youth, his mother was that rarity
of her time—a thoroughly educated woman—who introduced
her son to the classics of Occidental literature even before his
seventh birthday.

But as any dedicated L. Ron Hubbard reader will attest, his
world extended far beyond Montana. In point of fact, and as the
son of a United States naval officer, by the age of eighteen he
had traveled over a quarter of a million miles. Included therein
were three Pacific crossings to a then still mysterious Asia, where
he ran with the likes of Her British Majesty's agent-in-place

L. Ron Hubbard, left, at Congressional Airport, Washington, DC, 1931, with members of George Washington University flying club.

for North China, and the last in the line of Royal Magicians from the court of Kublai Khan. For the record, L. Ron Hubbard was also among the first Westerners to gain admittance to forbidden Tibetan monasteries below Manchuria, and his photographs of China's Great Wall long graced American geography texts.

Upon his return to the United States and a hasty completion of his interrupted high school education, the young Ron Hubbard entered George Washington University. There, as fans of his aerial adventures may have heard, he earned his wings as a pioneering barnstormer at the dawn of American aviation. He also earned a place in free-flight record books for the longest sustained flight above Chicago. Moreover, as a roving reporter for *Sportsman Pilot* (featuring his first professionally penned articles), he further helped inspire a generation of pilots who would take America to world airpower.

Immediately beyond his sophomore year, Ron embarked on the first of his famed ethnological expeditions, initially to then untrammeled Caribbean shores (descriptions of which would later fill a whole series of West Indies mystery-thrillers). That the Puerto Rican interior would also figure into the future of Ron Hubbard stories was likewise no accident. For in addition to cultural studies of the island, a 1932–33

LRH expedition is rightly remembered as conducting the first complete mineralogical survey of a Puerto Rico under United States jurisdiction.

There was many another adventure along this vein: As a lifetime member of the famed Explorers Club, L. Ron Hubbard charted North Pacific waters with the first shipboard radio direction finder, and so pioneered a long-range navigation system universally employed until the late twentieth century. While not to put too fine an edge on it, he also held a rare Master Mariner's license to pilot any vessel, of any tonnage in any ocean.

Yet lest we stray too far afield, there is an LRH note at this juncture in his saga, and it reads in part:

"I started out writing for the pulps, writing the best I knew, writing for every mag on the stands, slanting as well as I could."

To which one might add: His earliest submissions date from the summer of 1934, and included tales drawn from true-to-life Asian adventures, with characters roughly modeled on British/American intelligence operatives he had known in Shanghai. His early Westerns were similarly peppered with details drawn from personal experience. Although therein lay a first hard lesson from the often cruel world of the pulps. His first Westerns were soundly rejected as lacking the authenticity of a Max Brand yarn

Capt. L. Ron Hubbard in Ketchikan, Alaska, 1940, on his Alaskan Radio Experimental Expedition, the first of three voyages conducted under the Explorers Club flag.

(a particularly frustrating comment given L. Ron Hubbard's Westerns came straight from his Montana homeland, while Max Brand was a mediocre New York poet named Frederick Schiller Faust, who turned out implausible six-shooter tales from the terrace of an Italian villa).

Nevertheless, and needless to say, L. Ron Hubbard persevered and soon earned a reputation as among the most publishable names in pulp fiction, with a ninety percent placement rate of first-draft manuscripts. He was also among the most prolific, averaging between seventy and a hundred thousand words a month. Hence the rumors that L. Ron Hubbard had redesigned a typewriter for faster keyboard action and pounded out manuscripts on a continuous roll of butcher paper to save the precious seconds it took to insert a single sheet of paper into manual typewriters of the day.

That all L. Ron Hubbard stories did not run beneath said byline is yet another aspect of pulp fiction lore. That is, as publishers periodically rejected manuscripts from top-drawer authors if only to avoid paying top dollar, L. Ron Hubbard and company just as frequently replied with submissions under various pseudonyms. In Ron's case, the list

A MAN OF MANY NAMES

Between 1934 and 1950, L. Ron Hubbard authored more than fifteen million words of fiction in more than two hundred classic publications. To supply his fans and editors with stories across an array of genres and pulp titles, he adopted fifteen pseudonyms in addition to his already renowned L. Ron Hubbard byline.

Winchester Remington Colt
Lt. Jonathan Daly
Capt. Charles Gordon
Capt. L. Ron Hubbard
Bernard Hubbel
Michael Keith
Rene Lafayette
Legionnaire 148
Legionnaire 14830
Ken Martin
Scott Morgan
Lt. Scott Morgan
Kurt von Rachen
Barry Randolph
Capt. Humbert Reynolds

included: Rene Lafayette, Captain Charles Gordon, Lt. Scott Morgan and the notorious Kurt von Rachen—supposedly on the lam for a murder rap, while hammering out two-fisted prose in Argentina. The point: While L. Ron Hubbard as Ken Martin spun stories of Southeast Asian intrigue, LRH as Barry Randolph authored tales of

L. Ron Hubbard, circa 1930 , at the outset of a literary career that would finally span half a century.

romance on the Western range—which, stretching between a dozen genres is how he came to stand among the two hundred elite authors providing close to a million tales through the glory days of American Pulp Fiction.

In evidence of exactly that, by 1936 L. Ron Hubbard was literally leading pulp fiction's elite as president of New York's American Fiction Guild. Members included a veritable pulp hall of fame: Lester "Doc Savage" Dent, Walter "The Shadow" Gibson, and the legendary Dashiell Hammett—to cite but a few.

Also in evidence of just where L. Ron Hubbard stood within his first two years on the American pulp circuit: By the spring of 1937, he was ensconced in Hollywood, adopting a Caribbean thriller for Columbia Pictures, remembered today as *The Secret of Treasure Island*. Comprising fifteen thirty-minute episodes, the L. Ron Hubbard screenplay led to the most profitable matinée serial in Hollywood history. In accord with Hollywood culture, he was thereafter continually called

The 1937 Secret of Treasure Island, *a fifteen-episode serial adapted for the screen by L. Ron Hubbard from his novel,* Murder at Pirate Castle.

upon to rewrite/doctor scripts—most famously for long-time friend and fellow adventurer Clark Gable.

In the interim—and herein lies another distinctive chapter of the L. Ron Hubbard story—he continually worked to open Pulp Kingdom gates to up-and-coming authors. Or, for that matter, anyone who wished to write. It was a fairly unconventional stance, as markets were already thin and competition razor sharp. But the fact remains, it was an L. Ron Hubbard hallmark that he vehemently lobbied on behalf of young authors—regularly supplying instructional articles to trade journals, guest-lecturing to short story classes at George Washington University and Harvard, and even founding his own creative writing competition. It was established in 1940, dubbed the Golden Pen, and guaranteed winners both New York representation and publication in *Argosy*.

But it was John W. Campbell Jr.'s *Astounding Science Fiction* that finally proved the most memorable LRH vehicle. While every fan of L. Ron Hubbard's galactic epics undoubtedly knows the story, it nonetheless bears repeating: By late 1938, the pulp publishing magnate of Street & Smith was determined to revamp *Astounding Science Fiction* for broader readership. In particular, senior editorial director F. Orlin Tremaine called for stories with a stronger *human element*. When acting editor John W. Campbell balked, preferring his spaceship-driven tales,

Tremaine enlisted Hubbard. Hubbard, in turn, replied with the genre's first truly *character-driven* works, wherein heroes are pitted not against bug-eyed monsters but the mystery and majesty of deep space itself—and thus was launched the Golden Age of Science Fiction.

The names alone are enough to quicken the pulse of any science fiction aficionado, including LRH friend and protégé, Robert Heinlein, Isaac Asimov, A. E. van Vogt and Ray Bradbury. Moreover, when coupled with LRH stories of fantasy, we further come to what's rightly been described as the

foundation of every modern tale of horror: L. Ron Hubbard's immortal *Fear*. It was rightly proclaimed by Stephen King as one of the very few works to genuinely warrant that overworked term "classic"—as in: *"This is a classic tale of creeping, surreal menace and horror. . . . This is one of the really, really good ones."*

To accommodate the greater body of L. Ron Hubbard fantasies, Street & Smith inaugurated *Unknown*—a classic pulp if there ever was one, and wherein readers were soon thrilling to the likes of *Typewriter in the Sky* and *Slaves of Sleep* of which Frederik Pohl would declare: *"There are bits and pieces from Ron's work that became part of the language in ways that very few other writers managed."*

L. Ron Hubbard, 1948, among fellow science fiction luminaries at the World Science Fiction Convention in Toronto.

And, indeed, at J. W. Campbell Jr.'s insistence, Ron was regularly drawing on themes from the Arabian Nights and so introducing readers to a world of genies, jinn, Aladdin and Sinbad—all of which, of course, continue to float through cultural mythology to this day.

At least as influential in terms of post-apocalypse stories was L. Ron Hubbard's 1940 *Final Blackout*. Generally acclaimed as the finest anti-war novel of the decade and among the ten best works of the genre ever authored—here, too, was a tale that would live on in ways few other writers

imagined. Hence, the later Robert Heinlein verdict: "Final Blackout *is as perfect a piece of science fiction as has ever been written.*"

Like many another who both lived and wrote American pulp adventure, the war proved a tragic end to Ron's sojourn in the pulps. He served with distinction in four theaters and was highly decorated for commanding corvettes in the North Pacific. He was also grievously wounded in combat, lost many a close friend and colleague and thus resolved to say farewell to pulp fiction and devote himself to what it had supported these many years—namely, his serious research.

Portland, Oregon, 1943; L. Ron Hubbard captain of the US Navy subchaser PC 815.

But in no way was the LRH literary saga at an end, for as he wrote some thirty years later, in 1980:

"Recently there came a period when I had little to do. This was novel in a life so crammed with busy years, and I decided to amuse myself by writing a novel that was pure science fiction."

That work was *Battlefield Earth: A Saga of the Year 3000*. It was an immediate *New York Times* bestseller and, in fact, the first international science fiction blockbuster in decades. It was not, however, L. Ron Hubbard's magnum opus, as that distinction is generally reserved for his next and final work: The 1.2 million word *Mission Earth*.

> **Final Blackout**
> *is as perfect a piece of science fiction as has ever been written.*
>
> —Robert Heinlein

How he managed those 1.2 million words in just over twelve months is yet another piece of the L. Ron Hubbard legend. But the fact remains, he did indeed author a ten-volume *dekalogy* that lives in publishing history for the fact that each and every volume of the series was also a *New York Times* bestseller.

Moreover, as subsequent generations discovered L. Ron Hubbard through republished works and novelizations of his screenplays, the mere fact of his name on a cover signaled an international bestseller. . . . Until, to date, sales of his works exceed hundreds of millions, and he otherwise remains among the most enduring and widely read authors in literary history. Although as a final word on the tales of L. Ron Hubbard, perhaps it's enough to simply reiterate what editors told readers in the glory days of American Pulp Fiction:

He writes the way he does, brothers, because he's been there, seen it and done it!

THE STORIES FROM THE GOLDEN AGE

Your ticket to adventure starts here with the Stories from
the Golden Age collection by master storyteller L. Ron Hubbard.
These gripping tales are set in a kaleidoscope of exotic locales and brim
with fascinating characters, including some of the
most vile villains, dangerous dames and brazen heroes
you'll ever get to meet.

The entire collection of over one hundred and fifty stories is being
released in a series of eighty books and audiobooks.
For an up-to-date listing of available titles,
go to www.goldenagestories.com.

AIR ADVENTURE

Arctic Wings
The Battling Pilot
Boomerang Bomber
The Crate Killer
The Dive Bomber
Forbidden Gold
Hurtling Wings
The Lieutenant Takes the Sky

Man-Killers of the Air
On Blazing Wings
Red Death Over China
Sabotage in the Sky
Sky Birds Dare!
The Sky-Crasher
Trouble on His Wings
Wings Over Ethiopia

FAR-FLUNG ADVENTURE

SEA ADVENTURE

TALES FROM THE ORIENT

MYSTERY

FANTASY

SCIENCE FICTION

WESTERN

The Baron of Coyote River
Blood on His Spurs
Boss of the Lazy B
Branded Outlaw
Cattle King for a Day
Come and Get It
Death Waits at Sundown
Devil's Manhunt
The Ghost Town Gun-Ghost
Gun Boss of Tumbleweed
Gunman!
Gunman's Tally
The Gunner from Gehenna
Hoss Tamer
Johnny, the Town Tamer
King of the Gunmen
The Magic Quirt

Man for Breakfast
The No-Gun Gunhawk
The No-Gun Man
The Ranch That No One Would Buy
Reign of the Gila Monster
Ride 'Em, Cowboy
Ruin at Rio Piedras
Shadows from Boot Hill
Silent Pards
Six-Gun Caballero
Stacked Bullets
Stranger in Town
Tinhorn's Daughter
The Toughest Ranger
Under the Diehard Brand
Vengeance Is Mine!
When Gilhooly Was in Flower

JOIN THE PULP REVIVAL
America in the 1930s and 40s

Pulp fiction was in its heyday and 30 million readers were regularly riveted by the larger-than-life tales of master storyteller L. Ron Hubbard. For this was pulp fiction's golden age, when the writing was raw and every page packed a walloping punch.

That magic can now be yours. An evocative world of nefarious villains, exotic intrigues, courageous heroes and heroines—a world that today's cinema has barely tapped for tales of adventure and swashbucklers.

Enroll today in the Stories from the Golden Age Club and begin receiving your monthly feature edition selected from more than 150 stories in the collection.

You may choose to enjoy them as either a paperback or audiobook for the special membership price of $9.95 each month along with FREE shipping and handling.

CALL TOLL-FREE: 1-877-8GALAXY
(1-877-842-5299) OR GO ONLINE TO
www.goldenagestories.com
AND BECOME PART OF THE PULP REVIVAL!

Prices are set in US dollars only. For non-US residents, please call
1-323-466-7815 for pricing information. Free shipping available for US residents only.

Galaxy Press, 7051 Hollywood Blvd., Suite 200, Hollywood, CA 90028